D1043731

THE WRESTLING PRINCESS

If you were a king, would *you* be shocked if
your daughter drove a forklift truck? What if
she set out in armour to slay a dragon, or
wanted to be an astronaut? The kings in this
book are. *They* think princesses should behave
in true princessly fashion and settle down with
a suitably selected prince. Well, shouldn't
they?

The conventions of traditional fairy tales are
turned upside down in this witty collection of
splendid stories starring a new breed of
heroine — and hero!

"Corbalis's debut is as promising as Arthur
Ransome's many years ago with *Swallows and
Amazons*." *Spectator*

"Genuinely funny and written in a rollicking
style." *Northern Echo*

About the author

Judy Corbalis was born and brought up in
New Zealand. She first came to the UK on an
eighteen-month working holiday, but liked it
and stayed on. After attending the London
Academy of Music and Dramatic Art, she
worked in television, fringe and community
theatre, an opera company, and music hall –
both in the UK and New Zealand. *The
Wrestling Princess* is her first book and was
selected in the Feminist Book Fortnight 1986,
as one of their top 20 books of the year. Judy
currently lives in London and is working on a
number of other books for children.

The WRESTLING PRINCESS

and other stories

Judy Corbalis

Illustrations by Helen Craig

KNIGHT BOOKS
Hodder and Stoughton

For Toby, Jemima, Jerome,
Katya and Helen.

Text copyright © 1986 by Judy Corbalis
Illustrations copyright © 1986 by
Helen Craig

First Published in 1986 by
André Deutsch Ltd
This edition first published by
Knight Books 1987
Fifth impression 1988

*The characters and situations in this
book are entirely imaginary and
bear no relation to any real person
or actual happening.*

This book is sold subject to the
condition that it shall not, by way of
trade or otherwise, be lent, re-sold,
hired out or otherwise circulated
without the publisher's prior consent
in any form of binding or cover other
than that in which it is published and
without a similar condition including
this condition being imposed on the
subsequent purchaser.

No part of this publication may be
reproduced or transmitted in any
form or by any means, electronically
or mechanically, including
photocopying, recording or any
information storage or retrieval
system, without either the prior
permission in writing from the
publisher or a licence, permitting
restricted copying. In the United
Kingdom such licences are issued by
the Copyright Licensing Agency,
33–34 Alfred Place,
London. WC1E 7DP.

British Library C.I.P.

Corbalis, Judy.
The wrestling princess and other stories.
I. Title   II. Craig, Helen
823'.914[J]   PZ7

ISBN 0 340 40860 X

Printed and bound in Great Britain
for Hodder and Stoughton
Paperbacks, a division of Hodder and
Stoughton Ltd., Mill Road, Dunton
Green, Sevenoaks, Kent.
TN13 2YA.
(Editorial Office: 47 Bedford
Square, London WC1B 3DP) by
Cox & Wyman Ltd., Reading.

Contents

The
WRESTLING
PRINCESS

Once upon a time there was a princess who was six feet tall, who liked her own way and who loved to wrestle. Every day, she would challenge the guards at her father's palace to wrestling matches and every day, she won. Then she would pick up the loser and fling him on the ground, but gently, because she had a very kind nature.

The princess had one other unusual hobby. She liked to drive forklift trucks. Because she was a princess, and her father was very rich, she had three forklift trucks of her own – a blue one, a yellow one, and a green and purple striped one with a coronet on each side. Whenever there was a royal parade, the king would ride in front in his golden carriage, behind him would ride a company of soldiers and behind them came the princess driving her striped royal forklift truck. The king got very cross about it but the princess simply said, "If I can't drive my forklift truck, I won't go," and because she was such a good wrestler, the king was too scared to disagree with her.

One day, when the princess had wrestled with sixteen

soldiers at once and had beaten them all, the king sent a page to tell her to come to see him in the royal tea-room.

The princess was annoyed.

"Is it urgent?" she asked the page. "I was just greasing the axle of my blue forklift truck."

"I think you should come, Your Highness," said the page, respectfully, "His Majesty was in a terrible temper. He's burnt four pieces of toast already and dripped butter all over his second-best ermine robe."

"Oh gosh," said the princess, "I'd better come right away."

So she got up, picked up her oilcan and went into the royal bathroom to wash her hands for tea. She left oil marks all over the gold taps and the page sent a message to the palace housekeeper to clean them quickly before the king saw them.

The princess went down to the tea-room and knocked loudly on the door. A herald opened it. "The Princess Ermyntrude!" he announced.

"About time, too," said the king. "And where have you been?"

"Greasing the axle of the blue forklift truck," answered the princess politely.

The king put his head in his hands and groaned.

"This can't go on," he sighed tragically. "When *will* you stop messing about with these dirty machines, Ermyntrude? You're nearly sixteen and you need a husband. I must have a successor."

"I'll succeed you, father," cried the princess cheerfully. "I'd love to be a king."

"You can't be a king," said the king sadly. "It's not allowed."

"Why not?" asked the princess.

"I don't know," said the king. "I don't make the laws. Ask the judges — it's their affair. Anyway, you can't and that's that. You have to have a husband."

He picked up his tapestry and moodily started sewing.

"Ermyntrude," he said after a long silence, "you won't get a husband if you don't change your ways."

"Why ever not?" asked the princess, in surprise.

"To get a husband you must be enchantingly beautiful, dainty and weak," said the king.

"Well, I'm not," said Ermyntrude cheerfully. "I'm nothing to look at, I'm six feet tall and I'm certainly not weak. Why, Father, did you hear, this morning I wrestled with sixteen guards at once and I defeated them all?"

"Ermyntrude!" said the king sternly, as he rethreaded his needle with No. 9 blue tapestry cotton. "Ermyntrude, we are not having any more wrestling and no more forklift trucks either. If you want a husband, you will have to become delicate and frail."

"I *don't* want a husband," said the princess and she stamped her foot hard. The toast rack wobbled. "*You* want me to have a husband. I just want to go on wrestling and looking after my trucks and driving in parades."

"Well, you can't," said the king. "And that's that. I shall

lock up the forklift trucks and instruct the guards that there is to be no more wrestling and we shall have a contest to find you a husband."

The princess was furiously angry.

"Just you wait," she shouted rudely, "I'll ruin your stupid old contest. How dare you lock up my forklift trucks. You're a rotten mean old pig!"

"Ermyntrude," said the king sternly, putting down his tapestry, "you will do as you are told." And he got up and left the royal tea-room.

Princess Ermyntrude was very very angry. She bent the toasting fork in half and stamped on the bread.

"Stupid, stupid, stupid," she said crossly. And she went away to think out a plan.

The first contest to find a prince to marry the Princess Ermyntrude took place next day. The king had beamed a message by satellite to all the neighbouring countries, and helicopters with eligible princes in them were arriving in dozens at the palace heliport.

The princess watched them from the window of her room where she was sulking.

"Stupid, stupid," she said. "Why, not one of them even pilots his own helicopter."

And she went on sulking.

After lunch, the king sent a messenger to announce that the princess was to dress in her best robes and come to the great hall of the palace.

She put on her golden dress and her fur cape and her

small golden crown and her large golden shoes (for she had big feet) and down she went.

At the door of the throne room she stopped to give the herald time to announce her name, then she went in.

Seated inside were seventy-two princes, all seeking her hand in marriage.

The princess looked at them all. They all looked back.

"Sit here, my dear," said the king loudly, and under his breath, he added, "and behave yourself!"

The princess said nothing.

"Good afternoon and welcome to you all," began the king. "We are here today to find a suitable husband for the lovely Princess Ermyntrude, my daughter. The first competition in this contest will be that of height. As you know the princess is a very tall girl. She cannot have a husband shorter than herself so you will all line up while the Lord Chamberlain measures you."

The seventy-two princes lined up in six rows and the Lord Chamberlain took out the royal tape measure and began to measure them.

"Why can't I have a shorter husband?" whispered the princess.

"Be quiet. You just can't," said the king.

"Forty-eight princes left in the contest, Your Majesty," cried the Lord Chamberlain.

"Thank you," said the king. "I'm sorry you gentlemen had a wasted journey but you are welcome at the banquet this evening."

And he bowed very low.

"The second competition," said the king "will be that of disposition. The Princess Ermyntrude has a beautiful disposition, none better, but she does have a slightly hasty temper. She cannot have a husband who cannot match her temper. So we shall have a face-pulling, insult-throwing contest. The Lord Chamberlain will call your names one by one and you will come forward and confront the princess, pull the worst face you can manage, put on a temper display and insult her."

"Your Majesty, is this wise? Twenty-four of the princes have retired in confusion already," hissed the Lord Chamberlain.

"Weaklings," murmured the princess sweetly.

The first prince stepped forward. The Princess Ermyntrude pulled a repulsive face and he burst into tears.

"Eliminated," said the Lord Chamberlain running forward with a box of tissues. "Next!"

The next and the next after him and the prince following *them* were all eliminated and it was not until the fifth competitor crossed his eyes, stuck out his tongue and shouted, "Silly cry baby," at the princess, making her so angry that she forgot to shout back, that anyone succeeded at all.

The fifth prince inspired the next four after him but the princes after that were no match for Princess Ermyntrude until the eighteenth and nineteenth princes called her, "Crow face" and "Squiggle bum" and made her giggle.

By the end of the contest, there were seven princes left, all taller and more insulting than the princess.

"And now," said the king, "for the third and final contest. The third competition," he continued, "will be that of strength. As you may know, the Princess Ermyntrude is very strong. She cannot have a weaker husband so you will all line up and wrestle with her."

"Why can't I have a weaker husband?" whispered the princess.

"Be quiet. You just can't," said the king.

So the Lord Chamberlain lined up the seven princes and just as they were being given their instructions, the princess, who was flexing her arm muscles, glanced over at the watching crowd of commoners and noticed a short man covered in helicopter engine oil standing at the back. Because she was so tall, Princess Ermyntrude could see him clearly and, as she looked, he looked back at her and winked quite distinctly. The princess looked again. The short man winked again.

"*Helicopter* engine oil!" thought the princess. "That's the sort of man I like."

Just then the short man looked at her and, forming his mouth carefully, whispered silently, "Choose the seventh. Don't beat him."

The princess felt strangely excited. She looked again. The little man pointed discreetly to the tall, rather nervous looking prince at the end of the line-up. "That one," he mouthed.

Princess Ermyntrude didn't much like the look of the seventh prince but she did want to please the helicopter mechanic so she nodded discreetly, rolled up her golden sleeves and stepped forward to take on the first prince.

CRASH! He hit the mat with staggering force.

CRASH, CRASH, CRASH, CRASH, CRASH.

The next five princes followed. The poor seventh prince was looking paler and paler and his knees were beginning to buckle under him. The princess looked quickly at the mechanic who nodded briefly, then she moved towards the seventh prince. He seized her feebly by the arm.

"Good heavens, I could floor him with one blow," thought the princess, but she didn't. Instead, she let herself go limp and floppy and two seconds later, for the first time in her life, she lay flat on her back on the floor.

The crowd let out a stupendous cheer. The king and the Lord Chamberlain rushed forward and seized the hands of the young prince.

The poor prince looked very pale.

"This is terrible, terrible," he muttered desperately.

"Nonsense," cried the king. "I award you the hand of the princess and half my kingdom."

"But Sire . . ." stammered the prince. "I can't."

"Can't!" shouted the king. "What do you mean can't. You can and you will or I'll have you beheaded!"

There was a scuffle in the crowd and the helicopter mechanic darted forward and bent low at the king's feet.

"Majesty," he murmured reverently, "Majesty. I am the prince's helicopter pilot, mechanic and aide. Prince Florizel is overcome with shock and gratitude. Is that not so, Sire?" he asked turning to the prince.

"Um, yes, yes, that's right," said the prince nervously.

The mechanic smiled.

"Prince Florizel, of course, must have the blessing of *his* father, the King of Buzzaramia, whose kingdom adjoins your own, before the ceremony can take place. Is that not so, Sire?"

"Definitely," said the prince.

"Quite, quite," said the king, "I favour these old customs myself. The princess will fly there tomorrow to meet him, in her own royal helicopter."

"And I shall pilot myself," said the princess.

"We shan't go into *that* now," said the king. "Here, you may kiss the princess."

With a small sigh, the prince fainted dead away.

"Shock," said the pilot hastily. "Clearly shock, Your Majesty. It's not every day he wins the hand of such a beautiful, charming and talented young lady."

And he looked deep into the princess's eyes.

The prince was carried out to his helicopter and flown off by his pilot, with instructions that the Princess Ermyntrude would fly in the following day.

The rest of the contestants and the princess had a large and elegant banquet with a six-metre chocolate cake in the shape of a heart and litres of ice-cream.

"Who made that heart?" asked Ermyntrude.

"I ordered it from Cook," said the king.

"Well, *I* think it's soppy. A heart!" said the princess in disgust.

Next morning she was up early and, dressed in her frog-green flying suit and bright red aviator goggles, she slipped out to her helicopter before the king was up, climbed in and was just warming up the engine when the Lord Chamberlain came rushing out into the garden.

"Stop, stop," he cried waving his arms wildly. "Stop. His Majesty, your father, is coming too."

The Princess Ermyntrude turned off the master switch and leaned out of the window.

"Well, he'd better hurry and I'm piloting," she said carelessly. "I'll wait three minutes and I'm going if he hasn't come by then."

The Lord Chamberlain rushed into the palace and returned with the king hastily pulling his ermine robe over his nightshirt and replacing his nightcap with a crown.

"You're a dreadful girl, Ermyntrude," he said sadly. "Here I am with a hangover from the chocolate cake and you insist on being selfish."

"I'm *not* selfish," said Ermyntrude. "I'm by far the best pilot in the palace and it's your own fault you've got a hangover if you will encourage Cook to put rum in the chocolate cake. Anyway, all this was your idea. I'm not marrying that silly prince and I'm flying over to tell him so."

"Ermyntrude," cried the king, scandalized. "How can you do such a thing? I'll be ruined. He won the contest. And besides, you've got to marry someone."

"I haven't and I won't," said the princess firmly and she set the rotor blades in action.

Within an hour, they were flying into the next kingdom and soon they could see the palace shining golden on the highest hilltop.

"Over there," said the king mournfully. "Please change your mind, Ermyntrude."

"Never," said the princess positively. "Never, never, never, never, never."

Below them they could see the landing pad with ostrich feathers and fairy-lights along the strip.

Princess Ermyntrude settled the helicopter gently on the ground, waited for the blades to stop turning and got out.

The prince's mechanic was standing on the tarmac.

"A perfect landing," he cried admiringly.

The Princess Ermyntrude smiled. Just then, an older man in ermine trimmed pyjamas came running across the grass.

"Florizel, Florizel, what is all this?" he cried.

The mechanic picked up an oilcan from beside his feet.

"Put that down, you ninny," cried the man in ermine pyjamas. "Don't you know this is a royal princess?"

"You're being ridiculous, Father," said the mechanic. "Of course I know she's a princess. I'm going to marry her."

"*You* are?" cried Princess Ermyntrude's father. "My daughter's not marrying you. She's marrying your prince."

"I am marrying him," said the Princess Ermyntrude.

"She certainly is," said the mechanic. "And in case you're wondering, I *am* Prince Florizel. The other one was an imposter."

"But how?" asked the princess.

"Well," said Prince Florizel, "it was all my father's idea that I should go so I persuaded my mechanic to change places with me. I thought my father would never find out. Then, when I saw the Princess Ermyntrude, I fell instantly in love with her. She had axle grease on her neck and she was so big and strong. Then I realized it was lucky I'd changed places or you'd have eliminated me on height."

"That's right. You're too short," said the king.

"He's not," said the princess.

"No, I'm not, I'm exactly right and so is she," said Prince Florizel. "Then when I saw her pulling faces and shouting insults and throwing princes to the ground, I knew she was the one person I could fall in love with."

"Really?" asked the princess.

"Truly," said Prince Florizel. "Now, come and see my mechanical digger."

And holding the oilcan in one hand and the princess's hand in the other, he led the way to the machine shed.

The king looked at Prince Florizel's father.

"There's nothing I can do with her once she's made up her mind," he said wearily.

"I have the same trouble with Florizel," said the second king. "I say, would you like an Alka Seltzer and some breakfast?"

"Would I?" said the princess's father, "I certainly would."

So arm-in-arm they went off together to the palace.

And so Princess Ermyntrude and Prince Florizel were married in tremendous splendour.

The Princess Ermyntrude had a special diamond and gold thread boiler suit made for the wedding and she drove herself to the church in a beautiful bright red forklift truck with E in flashing lights on one side and F picked out in stars on the other and with garlands of flowers on the forks.

Prince Florizel, who had parachuted in for the wedding, wore an emerald and silver thread shirt with silver lamé trousers and had flowers in his beard. On the steps of the church he reached up on tiptoe to kiss the princess as the television cameras whirred and the people cheered, then they ran down the steps and jumped into the royal forklift and steered away through the excited crowds.

"I'm terribly happy," murmured the prince.

"So am I," said the princess. "I say did you bring the hamburgers and the ketchup?"

"All there in the back," said the prince.

"And I remembered the wedding cake. Look at it," said the princess proudly.

"Good heavens," cried Prince Florizel. "It's magnificent."

For the wedding cake was shaped like a giant oilcan.

"Perfect, don't you think?" murmured the princess.

"Absolutely," said the prince.

And they both lived happily ever after.

The
MAGIC
PARROT

Aunt Hilda was at home when Sam came in after school. He'd been hoping she'd be out but she was standing in the hallway with her beady black eyes snapping.

"Wipe your feet well," she said crossly. "Just look at the mud on your trousers."

Sam kept his hands behind his back.

"What have you got behind your back, Sam?" asked Aunt Hilda.

"Nothing," said Sam quickly, "Just a box, that's all."

"Nonsense!" Aunt Hilda was scornful. "Nobody goes round collecting empty boxes. What's in it?"

"Nothing," repeated Sam desperately.

"Well, put it on the hall table, then," she said, "and go in and get your tea quietly and quickly. I have a dreadful headache."

Aunt Hilda was always suffering from bad headaches. Sam had to be quiet in the house and tiptoe around and remember not to slam doors, and he could never ever have other children in to play because their noise might disturb Aunt Hilda and make her headaches worse.

He put his box down very carefully on the table and, crossing his fingers, he began to open the kitchen door.

Aunt Hilda looked at the box. Sam looked at Aunt Hilda. Very slowly the lid rose and a tiny brown face with little pointed ears and long long whiskers peeped out.

Aunt Hilda screamed and screamed. She rushed upstairs crying and shouting.

"Take it away! Get rid of it AT ONCE, you horrid, wicked boy."

Poor Sam seized the little hamster and, tucking it into his coat pocket, went into the kitchen and sadly ate his tea. The hamster climbed out of his pocket and sat on the table. Sam gave it some breadcrumbs and stroked its head. The hamster sat up and looked at him. Its fur was all soft and fluffy.

"She'll never let me keep it now," thought Sam. Then he wondered whether, if he promised to keep it in his room and never let it downstairs, Aunt Hilda and Uncle George might, just this once, let him have it after all.

He sat stroking the hamster for a long time until finally he heard Uncle George's key in the front door. He could hear voices on the stairs, Aunt Hilda's loud and angry, Uncle George's lower and soothing. Uncle George's footsteps came towards the kitchen. Sam put the hamster back in his pocket and put his hand over it to keep it safe.

The door opened.

Uncle George stood there looking very annoyed.

"Sam," he thundered, "I am extremely angry with you. You've upset your aunt and told her a lie. And you've brought a rodent into this house."

"It *isn't* a rodent," said Sam tearfully. "It's a baby hamster. This boy at school gave it to me. I'll look after it myself and it doesn't eat much and I'll pay for it out of my pocket money. *Please, please*, Uncle George."

"Certainly not. What an idea!" snorted Uncle George. "Hamsters *are* rodents: they're dirty and unpleasant and you're not keeping one here. Take it straight back to that boy! And as soon as you're home, go upstairs and apologise to your aunt."

And he went out.

Sam sat at the table looking at his hamster with tears in his eyes. He did want a pet so much. He wasn't allowed a dog or a cat, Uncle George had said a rabbit or a guinea pig would smell, and this hamster had seemed so perfect.

The hamster began to wash its face with its paws.

"I wish I could keep you," said Sam sadly. And he tucked it back in his pocket and slowly set off with it.

When he got home again, he went straight out to the far end of the back garden and climbed up the old apple tree. As he sat there feeling sad and lonely, he heard footsteps. Looking up at him was Blackbeard Smith, his aunt and uncle's gardener.

Blackbeard Smith lived in the big shed at the bottom of the garden. He kept the garden tidy and cleaned the car and did odd jobs round the house. Aunt Hilda didn't like him at all.

"It's ridiculous having a gardener like that. Of course he can't work properly," she used to say.

For the really interesting thing about Blackbeard Smith, apart from his wooden leg and the hook he had instead of a hand, was that he was a real live retired pirate. Sam had seen it on one of his letters once.

"B.B. Smith

Pirate (Retd.)".

Aunt Hilda had wanted to get rid of Blackbeard, but he came with the house.

"You can't do it, I'm afraid, my dear," Uncle George had said firmly.

Sam was strictly forbidden to go near Blackbeard's shed or to "bother" him at all but, in fact, he quite often talked to Blackbeard while the pirate was working in the garden, and he had a secret ambition to see inside his shed. Blackbeard was tall with a bushy beard and a glittering eye. Sam felt it would have been terrifying to have met him in his pirate clothes.

"Did you have a sword between your teeth?" he had asked Blackbeard once.

"Did I? Did I ever, young lad," roared Blackbeard. "A sword in me teeth and another in me hand and a revolver in me belt."

Sam had shuddered with fright at the thought.

Another mysterious thing about Blackbeard Smith was

where he went for his holidays. Every year, he would pack up a case and leave for a holiday. He always came back, but he would never say where he'd been. Aunt Hilda got very cross.

"How ridiculous," she said. "Of course we should know where he's going. What if there's an emergency?"

But there never was and Blackbeard Smith would never tell.

"I'm staying with an old friend," was all he would say.

Sam looked at the pirate through the branches.

Blackbeard Smith winked up at him.

"It's a beautiful evening," he called cheerily.

Sam glowered down. "No, it's not."

Blackbeard Smith ran his hook menacingly across the tree trunk.

"Sulking, are we?" he enquired. "Moody, are we? What's on our mind, then? Come down and tell the scourge of the South Sea Clippers what the matter is."

Sam crawled unhappily down the tree trunk.

"I'm in the wrong family," he muttered gloomily. "I hate them."

"One way or another," said Blackbeard Smith, "we're all in the wrong family. So what's the problem with them now?"

"They won't let me keep my hamster," blurted out Sam, and he began to cry. "I haven't got *any* pets. Not a white mouse, not a kitten, not nothing."

"Not *anything*," corrected Blackbeard. "You may not

have a pet, you may be disappointed in life, but for goodness' sake speak proper, boy."

Sam sniffed.

"You'd better come in and sit down and we'll see what we can come up with," said Blackbeard, and he led Sam into his big shed.

This was the moment Sam had been waiting for for months.

They stepped inside and Sam saw that the shed was divided into three rooms. Blackbeard pushed open a door and Sam was inside the first retired pirate's sitting room he'd ever seen in his life.

"I don't believe it," he breathed.

"Look around, look around," said Blackbeard expansively. "I'll just go off and slip into something more comfortable."

And while Sam tried the telescope and inspected the room generally, the old pirate stumped off to his back room.

Five minutes later he was back.

"Incredible!" cried Sam.

"And this," announced Blackbeard Smith grandly, pulling a photograph from behind the armadillo shell, "is my former parrot, Cocky Smart, Retired."

"Retired where?" Sam was curious.

"Where?" cried Blackbeard Smith. "This boy asks me where! Now where would you think a parrot would retire to? Eastbourne? Too northerly! Blackpool? Too political!

Weymouth? Too many day trippers! Chipping Sodbury? Too rural! The Zoo? Of course not! Use your intelligence, boy. Where would a parrot retire to?"

"I don't know," said poor Sam.

"The West Indies, of course. Where else? Set himself up nicely in a banana tree near Kingston. Got himself a pretty wife and a fine clutch of eggs, which hatched into a colourful family of six."

"And that's where you go every year!"

"Of course, boy," boomed Blackbeard Smith. "Every summer, it's off to the West Indies to spend a month with Cocky Smart. Now there's not many retired pirates can boast they're invited by their former parrots to spend the summer holidays, I can tell you."

Sam was impressed.

"He looks very nice," he said, looking at the parrot's photograph. "Look at the way he's looking at you. That's the kind of pet *I'd* like."

Blackbeard Smith struck a match against his wooden leg and lit his pipe thoughtfully.

"And why shouldn't you?" he asked after a while. "And why not, then? Mind, it would have to be specially worked out. Go home now, boy, and apologise to your aunt, and come down here and see me this time tomorrow."

Sam could hardly wait. He arrived promptly at Blackbeard's shed next day and knocked on the door. Blackbeard took him into the marvellous sitting room and handed him a glass.

"Have a quick shot of this, boy," he said. "Afternoon tea."

And he winked at Sam.

Sam swallowed a large mouthful. A terrible burning seized his throat. He coughed and spat and spluttered.

"What is it?"

"Rum, boy, rum," said the old pirate. "Builds growing boys. Now if you just sit tight here I've got something next door you're going to be very pleased to see."

Sam sat down gratefully. He was feeling rather dizzy from the effects of the rum.

"Close your eyes," shouted Blackbeard from outside the door.

Sam's eyes were already shut. The rum had made them sting.

"Open them now!"

Sam decided he was feeling better. He opened his eyes cautiously and saw, sitting on the pirate's shoulder, a strange object covered by a tea towel.

"Pull it off, boy," growled Blackbeard Smith. Sam lifted off the tea towel.

Underneath sat a beautiful shiny metal parrot.

"Oh!" cried Sam, "IT'S WONDERFUL."

"He's yours," said Blackbeard Smith.

And he lifted the parrot onto Sam's shoulder.

"Made him meself last night. Have a good close look at him now."

Sam was overjoyed.

"He's fantastic. I love him. Oh thank you, Blackbeard, thank you."

"Just take good care of him, that's all," muttered the old pirate. "Now off you go. I've got summer holiday packing to do. Can't find me spare hook anywhere."

Sam went racing out to the street, his parrot on his shoulder.

"Look, everybody, look!" he shouted. "*I've* got a pet. A fantastic parrot."

Sam's parrot was a great success. He took him to school next morning.

"His name's Achilles," he told his friends at morning playtime and they all took turns at stroking the parrot.

"Where did you get him?" asked David.

"It's a secret," said Sam. "But I can tell you a man I know gave him to me."

Achilles' fame spread.

After school everyone wanted to walk home with Sam and carry Achilles for him. Sam kept Achilles firmly on his own shoulder.

"He's new to me," he explained. "He has to get used to me. I can't go handing him round to everyone, or he'll get frightened."

"Can I come to tea?" asked David when they got to Sam's gate.

Sam hesitated. He was longing to have David in and to show off Achilles and let him meet Blackbeard Smith. But he remembered Aunt Hilda's cross look and thought better of it.

"I'm not allowed to have people to tea," he said. "It's my aunt. She gets headaches easily."

David was disappointed.

"Well, bring Achilles out later," he said. "And let me have *one* turn with him. I am supposed to be your best friend, after all."

"You are," Sam assured him.

He took Achilles out after tea and they took turns with him on their shoulders. When he got home, Sam saw Blackbeard in the garden. He and Achilles rushed down to the shed.

"Look, Blackbeard," cried Sam. "He's really good. Everybody likes him and he sits on *my* shoulder all the time and look at how he looks at me. Just like Cocky Smart."

"And what does your aunt say, then?" queried the pirate.

"*She* thinks he's just a toy. She doesn't know he's a real pet," said Sam.

"All to the good, boy," remarked Blackbeard Smith. "And I shouldn't tell her meself if I were you. Now, I'm off early tomorrow morning and when I come back there'll be a present from Jamaica for you. Take care of that parrot while I'm gone."

"Oh, I will!" Sam assured him. "Have a good holiday, Blackbeard."

The pirate waved his hook and disappeared into his shed.

Sam took Achilles up to his room and sat him on the wooden bed-end.

"There's your perch," he said. "You can sleep there."

He smiled at Achilles.

Achilles winked at him.

Sam's eyes opened wide. He couldn't possibly have seen properly.

Achilles winked again.

"Achilles!" whispered Sam softly. "Wink again."

Achilles winked.

"Go to sleep," breathed Sam.

Achilles obediently put his head under his wing.

Sam climbed into bed and fell asleep.

Next day at school he told David that Achilles could wink.

"I don't believe that." David was scornful. "He's a really good parrot but he's made of metal and he can't wink."

"He can, he can," said Sam. "At playtime I'll show you."

But Achilles refused to wink or move his head and no one believed Sam at all.

That night, Sam put Achilles on the bed-end.

"Wink!" he ordered.

Achilles winked.

"Put your head under your wing," said Sam.

Achilles did.

"He only does it with him and me around," Sam said to himself. "And I suppose maybe he'll do it with Blackbeard Smith as well, when he's back from his holiday."

Things went very nicely for the next week or so. Quite a lot of children asked Sam to tea and they all loved Achilles.

But at the end of the week something dreadful happened. It started very surprisingly.

One night Sam and Achilles went to bed as usual. Sam had been asleep for quite a long time when he was suddenly awoken by strange noises. He opened his eyes and peeped cautiously out from under the covers.

Achilles was sitting up on the end of the bed.

"Hallo, Sam," he said. He had a very creaky metal voice.

"*HALLO!*" replied Sam. "You can *talk*."

"I've been listening to you and learning," creaked Achilles. "All parrots should be able to talk. And I've been singing."

"So that's what the noises were," thought Sam.

"I'm not very good yet. I'm practising," explained Achilles. "But it's used up all my energy. I'm hungry, Sam."

Sam lifted Achilles onto his shoulder and crept down to the kitchen with him.

And it was while he was searching in the cupboard for some bread and cheese for Achilles that the dreadful thing happened.

Achilles gave a creaky squawk of joy, and Sam turned

round just in time to see him eating the knobs off the cooker. As Sam watched in horror, he reached out and pecked off the door handle.

"Achilles!" cried Sam in a loud whisper. "Stop it *at once!* What are you doing?"

"Mmmmm," croaked Achilles dreamily. "Delicious. Yum, yum."

And he patted his stomach contentedly with his wing.

Sam looked at the cooker, seized Achilles and rushed back up to bed as fast as he could.

Next morning there was an awful commotion.

"But how could it have happened?" asked Uncle George.

"I keep telling you I don't know, but you don't hear me." Aunt Hilda was exasperated. "What I can tell you is that it *has* happened and I can't use the cooker anymore."

That night, as Sam lay in bed after his Chinese takeaway supper, he heard scuffling and creaking from the end of the bed. Sitting up, he saw Achilles climb off the bed and creep across the floor and out of the door.

Sam followed him. Somehow he thought Achilles seemed bigger and fatter. The parrot waddled into the kitchen and over to the washing machine, opened his beak, and snap, snap, he swallowed all the washing machine buttons.

Sam was horrified.

"Come *here*, Achilles," he whispered.

Achilles came creaking over to him.

"You're not to eat up anything in this kitchen," explained

Sam. "We need all the buttons and knobs and things. Please, Achilles."

Achilles dreamily lifted the cheese grater off its hook with his wing and swallowed it down.

"But I was hungry," he croaked.

Sam gave a sigh, picked him up and went back to bed.

When he woke up next morning, he took Achilles onto his shoulder. The parrot was definitely heavier and taller than he had been the day before.

"Achilles," said Sam, "all this food is making you grow. You'll be too big to sit on my shoulder if you go on eating. You've got to stop."

That night, after his Indian takeaway supper, he measured Achilles. He was five centimetres taller!

"Achilles," said Sam sternly, "YOU ARE NOT TO GO DOWN TO THE KITCHEN TONIGHT AND STEAL THINGS. Do you promise?"

Achilles put his wing on his heart.

"I promise, Sam."

Sam was woken next morning by loud shouts of dismay from his uncle and aunt's room.

"All the taps in the bathroom are missing," shouted his uncle.

"*And* the cabinet doorknobs," sobbed his aunt.

"I can't have a bath!" roared Uncle George.

"This house is haunted," wept Aunt Hilda.

Sam looked at Achilles.

Achilles was even bigger.

"You promised," he reminded him sadly.

"I know," squawked Achilles, "and I was very good. I didn't go *near* the kitchen although the cabinet doorknobs there are much bigger and I was starving."

Sam put his head in his hands. He wished Blackbeard Smith would come back soon.

Achilles wiggled his metal feathers and stroked Sam's cheek with his beak.

"I love you, Sam," he creaked.

"I know," said Sam sadly.

All day in school he couldn't concentrate. He had left Achilles hidden under the bed. Achilles was getting so much bigger, Sam couldn't carry him anywhere on his shoulder any more.

What could he do?

And Blackbeard Smith was still on holiday!

"Maybe," thought Sam, "he'll have arrived home when I get back from school today."

But as soon as he turned into his own street, he saw that something bad had happened. His uncle was standing by the gate, looking thunderous, talking to a large policeman. Sam's heart sank.

"What's happened?" he asked nervously.

"I don't know what's happening," his uncle said grimly, "but I intend to find out. Now someone's taken the lawnmower."

"But it was locked in the shed." said Sam, knowing exactly who it would be.

"That's right," said his uncle. "And it's too big to get out through the window."

Sam raced into the house and upstairs. Achilles was lying under the bed.

"Come out, *at once*," he cried.

Achilles wriggled out from under. He was at least twenty centimetres taller!

"Achilles!" shouted Sam. "*You* ate that lawnmower."

Achilles hung his head. His beak trembled.

"I know," he whispered. "I was terribly hungry."

Sam was distraught.

"Oh, Achilles, what shall I *do* with you?"

"I don't know," said Achilles humbly. "I get so hungry I can't help myself. That lawnmower was delicious. I won't need to eat again for ages."

Sam looked at him.

"If you eat any more," he warned, "you won't be able to fit under my bed and you'll have to stay outside."

An oily tear trickled down Achilles' face.

"I don't want to stay outside by myself."

"Well, STOP EATING!"

Sam picked up his football.

"I'm going out and you're not coming with me," he said. "You're staying inside. You're getting too big for my shoulder."

But Achilles looked so sad that Sam felt sorry for him and decided to carry him into the garden for a bit.

He left his parrot hidden behind the garden shed and went off to play football.

He and his friends had been playing for about an hour when they heard a lot of noise and saw an odd procession of people coming towards the park.

At the front was a very fat, very angry woman with a small boy crying loudly beside her, and behind them came three more children, two boys on bicycles, two mothers, three fathers, a tramp, a policeman, Sam's uncle, another half dozen children, four dogs and a big tom cat. And right at the back, Sam saw, with a sinking heart, a strangely familiar figure wrapped in a large old gardening coat and cap. It was Achilles! He had gone out by himself for the first time.

The procession came into the park. The very fat woman was shouting angrily and waving her fists. Sam went up to her.

"What's the matter?" he asked.

"Matter!" shouted the woman. "I'll tell you what's the matter. Somebody's stolen his tricycle! That's what's the matter. We're all looking for the thief and when we catch him, I'll make him sorry, I can tell you."

Sam seized his football and joined the procession behind Achilles.

As soon as he could he pulled Achilles to one side.

"I was just helping them look," explained the parrot.

"Achilles!" Sam was angry. "You're telling me a lie. *You* ate that tricycle."

Achilles was embarrassed.

"How did you know?"

"Look at yourself, you stupid parrot!" shouted Sam.

"I'm not a stupid parrot," sobbed Achilles. "You said I was a fantastic parrot. And I know I'm a very hungry parrot."

"Well, you're not a fantastic parrot now. You're an enormous parrot with wheels coming out of your shoulders," cried Sam in despair. "I don't know what to feed you with, and I can't keep people from knowing it's

you doing all these things for much longer."

"You don't love me any more," wept Achilles. "Just because I'm hungry and I've got too big. I don't mean to eat up things. They look so delicious, and I'm always starving. Please help me, Sam."

"I don't know how to help you," explained Sam.

"But you're clever," said Achilles. "You can read and add up."

"We'd better go home," said Sam, "and see if Blackbeard Smith's back from holiday. Maybe he can suggest something."

But Blackbeard Smith was still away.

"You'll have to go in the tool shed," said Sam. "I'm really sorry, Achilles. Wait here and I'll get the key. I daren't risk taking you inside."

For Achilles was now taller than Sam.

"I'm scared of the dark," muttered Achilles.

"I'll bring you my torch," promised Sam, "and tomorrow I'll try to think of something to do."

By the time Sam got back with the key and the torch, Achilles had eaten the incinerator that was kept beside the shed, and was another fifteen centimetres taller.

"Kiss me goodnight," begged the parrot.

"I can't reach your beak," said Sam sadly.

With a lot of creaks and clangs, Achilles bent down. Sam kissed his beak and went inside to bed.

He tossed and turned all night long and slept very badly.

Next day he decided not to go to school.

"I've got a very sore throat," he told his aunt.

"Measles, I expect," she said grimly. "Well, I'm going out this morning. You'll have to stay here by yourself."

Sam was overjoyed. It would make getting the parrot out of the garden much simpler.

But where could he put Achilles? He went out to the tool shed as soon as his aunt had left.

Achilles was delighted to see him and stroked Sam's head with his metal wing.

"You've thought of something?" he creaked hopefully.

"Well, not exactly. I'm just sorting something out," said Sam untruthfully. "First, we have to get you out of the garden."

He draped the coat round Achilles and pulled the cap low down over his beak, then together they set off down the street. Sam had no idea where he was going, but headed vaguely in the direction of the park. Suddenly, ahead of them, Sam saw a policeman. Quick as a flash, he pulled Achilles down onto a low brick wall and sat beside him.

"Keep your head down," he hissed.

The policeman stopped and looked at them with mild interest.

"Good morning," he said.

"Good morning," creaked Achilles.

"It's my grandpa," said Sam desperately. "He's got a bad chest."

"What a shame," said the sympathetic policeman, and walked on.

Then, as Sam sat racking his brains, he had a sudden wonderful idea!

"Get up quickly, Achilles, we're going to the park."

They got to the park and Sam looked cautiously round for a suitable spot.

"Over there," he decided.

He took Achilles to an empty space amongst the trees, pulled off the coat and told the parrot to take off the cap.

"Now just stand here," ordered Sam.

"But everyone will see me," objected Achilles.

"EXACTLY!" cried Sam. "They'll think you're a piece of park sculpture. You're quite safe here and I can go away and try to sort out something. Now, you must promise to stay right here."

"Yes."

"And you won't move away?"

"I promise."

"Good," said Sam. "I'll be back in about an hour."

And he set off to find a solution.

He wandered round the streets for a long time trying to

think of something, but by the time he returned to the park he still had no idea what to do about Achilles.

As he got near the open space where he had left the parrot, he noticed a crowd of people gathering. Feeling rather uneasy, he pushed his way through.

Achilles was still standing where Sam had left him, but he had clearly been away. Out of his head gushed a bright jet of water. While Sam had been gone, he had eaten the park fountain!

"But that sculpture wasn't there yesterday," insisted a woman at the front of the crowd.

"Keep still," hissed Sam to Achilles. "Stand still."

"I *am* standing still," said the man next door to Sam.

The crowd continued to argue about the new statue. Things were becoming rather heated when there was a sudden shout from behind them.

"Look out! Look out! Danger!"

Sam couldn't see what was going on, but the voice continued.

"Run, run, the new electronic mechanical digger's gone out of control and its heading this way!"

The crowd of people scattered in all directions.

Sam looked at Achilles.

"Put me on your shoulder," he ordered. "Hurry!"

Achilles lifted Sam in his beak and set him on his shoulder.

The digger was quite far off but advancing quickly. You could see where it had been by the trail it was cutting through the park. As Sam watched, it veered to the left, tore down the park gates, and set off along the street, ripping up large chunks of the road as it went. People ran screaming away from it.

"What is it?" asked Achilles.

"It's a digger," explained Sam, "and its electronic brain has gone wrong."

"It looks *delicious*," said Achilles. "And I'm starving again."

And with Sam clinging to his neck feathers, he lumbered off after the digger.

As they went along, Sam realised in horror that the digger was heading out of the park and towards his own street.

Achilles, who was getting hungrier and hungrier, ran faster and faster.

"I wish that pirate had made me with longer wings, and I could fly," he panted.

As they drew closer, Sam saw that the digger had begun to swerve and that it was tearing up the fence round his aunt and uncle's garden.

Aunt Hilda leant out of the top-floor window, shouting and screaming.

"Help, help! I'll be killed! It's coming straight for me. Oh help, someone!"

The digger dug up the rose garden. It was coming towards the house.

"Hurry, hurry, Achilles!" cried Sam.

Achilles leapt forward on his enormous feet. He opened his great beak.

CRUNCH!

He bit off the digger's metal jaws.

CRUNCH! CRUNCH!

He bit off the digger's mechanical arm.

CRUNCH! CRUNCH! CRUNCH!

He gobbled up the digger's caterpillar tracks and half of the empty cab.

And while Aunt Hilda watched in astonishment, he chewed up all the rest of it.

The mechanical digger was completely eaten up.

"Sam," said Achilles, "that was the best meal I've eaten yet. I have to sit down to digest it."

Aunt Hilda threw open the window.

"Is that you, Sam?" she called.

Sam's heart sank.

"Yes," he answered nervously.

"You wonderful, clever, amazing boy," cried Aunt Hilda. "You've saved my life!"

She rushed out of the door and ran across the garden.

"Oh, Sam, how can I ever thank you enough," she cried gratefully. "You're to choose anything you want, anything at all."

Just at that moment, there came the sound of a familiar voice.

"Is anybody at home to greet the Terror of the Tearing Tea-clippers?" it shouted. "Come out, or I'll carve ye up

with me hook."

And there, behind Sam, appeared Blackbeard Smith. He looked down at Achilles who was fast asleep after his enormous meal.

"Having a little trouble, are we?" he enquired genially. "Something gone a little bit wrong somewhere has it, then?"

And taking an oil can in his hook, he dropped three drops onto Achilles' tail feathers, adjusted a knob somewhere in Achilles' chest and turned a screw in his head feathers.

There was a clanging and grinding and a sudden rushing clunk! And Achilles shrank back to his old size.

"Oh, Blackbeard!" cried Sam. "He's normal again. He's fixed."

"Quite himself, I can tell you," muttered the pirate. "Been eating, has he?"

"Everything, just everything," Sam said. "And there was nothing I could do."

He bent down and picked up Achilles in his arms.

"He's cured now," said Blackbeard Smith. "It won't happen again, ye may be sure."

At that moment Aunt Hilda who had been inspecting the damaged fence, noticed the pirate.

"Mr. Smith," she said, with a warm smile. "How was your holiday? I'm delighted to see you back. We do miss your services in the garden, you know."

Blackbeard Smith looked hard at Sam.

"This brave boy," continued Aunt Hilda, "has just saved me from a frightful death. I was lying down with a headache when I heard a terrible noise and saw that dreadful machine coming straight at the house."

"Cured your headache, ma'am, without doubt," murmured Blackbeard Smith.

"I shall never have a headache again," said Aunt Hilda decidedly. "And Sam is to choose anything he wants as a reward."

"Anything?" asked Sam.

"Anything at all," answered his aunt.

"Choose carefully now, boy," said the pirate.

"Well," said Sam, thinking hard, "first, I'd like to be allowed friends to tea, and friends *I* choose."

"Of course," said Aunt Hilda.

"Then," Sam went on, "I want to be allowed to go into Blackbeard Smith's shed any time he says I can."

"Certainly," replied Aunt Hilda.

"And, last of all, I want to be allowed as many pets as I want."

Aunt Hilda swallowed hard.

"Well . . . ," she said.

"You promised," Sam reminded her.

"Yes," said Aunt Hilda, "I did promise. And you can. I shall speak to Uncle George about it tonight."

"Very lucky that. Nice piece of timing there," said Blackbeard Smith. "Because it just so happens I brought the young hero a little present from Jamaica."

And he pulled a box out of his coat pocket.

Sam opened the box. Inside was a tortoise.

"Oh Blackbeard!" cried Sam, "I've always wanted a tortoise."

"And one or two other things," said the pirate, "which we'll deal with later. Meanwhile here's a shell which sings if you hold it to your ear."

"It is a rather beautiful tortoise," said Aunt Hilda. "I feel I could probably get to like it in time. But I do think we should go inside now and have some tea."

"Aunt Hilda," said Sam, "I've decided to ask someone to tea today."

"Today?" said his aunt.

"Yes, today," repeated Sam. "I want Blackbeard Smith to come to tea."

"Of course, dear," said his aunt. "Mr. Smith will be very welcome."

They went into the kitchen and sat down at the table.

"Sam," said Aunt Hilda, "as it's such a special day today and you have a friend to tea, I've decided to go out and buy icecream and cake."

"Oh, thank you," cried Sam, and he gave Aunt Hilda a kiss.

Aunt Hilda was very pleased. She took her purse and went out.

Blackbeard Smith and Sam were left alone together. Achilles was still asleep on Sam's shoulder. Sam's tortoise was sitting on his knee.

"It's been a busy time, I see," remarked the retired pirate.

"I've been waiting every day for you to come back," said Sam.

"Sorry ye've had so much trouble with him, boy," said the pirate. "But he's all right now."

"Blackbeard," said Sam, "have you ever owned a dog?"

"Dog?" The pirate looked interested. "Of course I've had a dog. A sea-faring dog that was tied to the mast in the storms of the Indian Ocean. There's nothing about dogs Blackbeard Smith don't know. Remarkable dog I had, and many's the time Cocky Smart rode on his back."

"Do you think I could train Achilles to ride on a dog's back if I had one?"

"Undeniably, boy. That bird can be trained to do anything."

"When I get my dog, Blackbeard," asked Sam, "will you show me how to train him?"

Blackbeard rested his hook on Sam's shoulder. "Without doubt, boy. Without doubt. We'll begin discussing it right away."

And they were still discussing it when Aunt Hilda came back with the icecream and cake, a bottle of rum for Blackbeard Smith, and a packet of birdseed for Achilles.

"A kind thought, ma'am," said the pirate, "but that bird don't touch birdseed. A few drops of 3-in-1 oil will do him fine."

Achilles opened his eyes and looked around hungrily.

Aunt Hilda went to the cupboard under the sink, took out the bicycle oil, put a little in her saucer and gave it to him.

Achilles looked at Sam.

"Can I?"

"Can he?" Sam asked Blackbeard.

"Of course he can," said the pirate. "Cocky Smart's favourite tipple is marshmallow flavoured coconut oil."

Achilles dipped his beak into the saucer and gave a deep sigh of contentment.

"You know something?" Sam said to Blackbeard and Aunt Hilda. "However many pets I get, my favourite will always be Achilles."

And Achilles snuggled comfortably into Sam's neck and lovingly pecked his ear.

ARSINOEE
and the
GREBBLE

One day appeared upon the roads
Of friendly Hertfordshire
A monstrous thing that breathed out smoke
And set the towns on fire.

It made its scaly lumbrous way
Across each field and wood
And burnt down crops and trees and barns
And houses where they stood.

It swallowed cows and stable boys
And hens and pigs for food
And every little child it met
It gobbled up and chewed.

It burned down Bushey, Radlett, Mimms,
It chewed up Brookmans Park,
Then headed off across the fields
To Swipping-in-the-Nark.

Now Swipping, as you're sure to know,
Is very, very small.
It only has five shops, a church,
A pub and village hall.

And when the Swipping villagers
Were told by Scotland Yard
The grebble was approaching them,
They took it very hard.

"Our church is mediaeval,"
Sighed the Reverend Cuthbert Stone.
"Imagine if it eats the font!"
He gave a hollow moan.

Miss Gilbertson, the postmistress,
Who kept the general store
Was told the news and fainted
Dead away upon the floor.

"I'm sorry," said Inspector Grey,
"The news is very sad.
It's certainly approaching here
And things look rather bad."

"But surely, sir," cried Dr. Brown
"The Yard will stop this pillage.
You cannot let this ugly thing
Destroy our pretty village."

"I'm sorry," the inspector said,
"But what I've said is true.
The grebble is a frightful beast:
There's nothing we can do."

The villagers were so dismayed
That, in the village square,
They called a meeting. Everyone
For miles around was there.

"Has anyone a plan at all?"
The Reverend Cuthbert cried.
"We must destroy this fearful beast!"
But nobody replied.

There was a most unusual child,
By name, Arsinoee.
She said, "It's time that awful thing
Came face to face with *me*."

Arsinoee was round and fair,
Her eyes were small and pink:
She had a very clever brain.
She switched it on to THINK.

"I think," said sweet Arsinoee,
"I have a clever plan.
I think that I will trap that beast
I'm certain that I can."

"You couldn't, dear. You're just a child,"
The village doctor said.
Arsinoee replied with heat,
"You go and boil your head!

You're far too old: your brain's worn out.
You leave this job to me."
The villagers, aghast, replied,
"Just let her wait and see.

The grebble's bound to eat her up
And, as she is so rude,
It serves her right if she ends up
As gobbled grebble food."

But one of them cried, "Let her try!
Her eyes are small and pink,
And everybody knows that that
Will mean that she can think."

Arsinoee went home and got
Some marbles, rope and ham,
A capgun, soap, a loaf of bread,
And bubblegum and jam.

She stretched the rope beneath some trees,
Spread marbles on the ground,
Put down the soap and laid the food
Together in a mound.

A sudden rumble sounded near,
The birds flew off in fright,
The trees and buildings bent and shook.
THE GREBBLE CAME IN SIGHT!

Arsinoee was not afraid.
She stood out in the square
And shouted, "Hey, you ugly beast!
Arsinoee is here!"

The grebble roared a mighty roar,
Arsinoee stood calm.
"I'll eat you up!" the monster screamed.
Arsinoee said, "Garn!

"You couldn't eat a rotten egg,
You couldn't fight a flea,
And even if YOU think you're wild
You simply don't scare me."

The grebble reared its ugly head
And fixed her with its eye.
Arsinoee looked bravely back,
And all she said was, "Hi!"

The monster rushed towards the girl,
(She stood beside the bread),
It lumbered onwards, breathing fire,
Then smelt the food ahead.

"Ah! BREAD AND JAM!" the grebble cried.
"My very favourite food!
I'll have you for the second course
Although it's rather rude."

It made a dash towards the food
But slipped upon the soap,
Then on the marbles slid about
And tripped across the rope.

It lay there on the village street,
Arsinoee came by.
She blew a bubble from her gum
And glued the grebble's eye.

"Help! Help!" the monster cried in fright.
"It's gone as dark as night."
Arsinoee took out the rope
And tied the grebble tight.

She held the capgun in her hand
And stood beside its head.
"Look out!" she said. "I've got a gun:
I'm going to shoot you dead."

"No! No!" the grebble sobbed in fear,
"I'm sorry I was bad.
I had no bread and jam to eat
I went a little mad."

"You're very bad. I ought to shoot.
I really think I should."
The grebble cried, "Arsinoee,
I promise to be good.

Don't shoot me please. I won't be bad
I really will be good.
I'll clean your house and make your tea
And carry coal and wood."

Arsinoee thought long and hard.
She said, "It seems a shame.
At least I ought to let you try.
Perhaps you weren't to blame.

I'll take you home and try it out.
You'll have to be polite,
And clean the house and give me rides
And stay inside at night."

"I will! I will!" the grebble cried.
"I'll carry you around."
Arsinoee climbed on its back.
It got up off the ground.

Along the village street they went;
She gave a mighty shout.
"I've stopped the grebble. Now it's safe
Come on, you cowards, come out!"

ARSINOEE AND THE GREBBLE

The villagers were all amazed.
"You clever thing!" they said.
"I've got pink eyes," the girl replied.
"I really use my head.

I'm going to take this monster home.
(We're just in time for tea.)
Next time you need a problem solved
You'd better send for me."

The grebble is in Swipping still,
It's with Arsinoee.
It never roars or breathes out fire
Or makes the people flee.

It likes to help Arsinoee
In every way it can
And, in return, she always feeds it
Lots of bread and jam.

VIOLET KATZ
and the
PINK ELEPHANT

One morning Violet Katz woke up and saw a pink elephant looking in at her window.

"Ma," shrieked Violet Katz, "there's a pink elephant outside my window!"

Downstairs Mrs. Katz was stirring the porridge.

"Don't be ridiculous, Violet," she shouted upstairs.

"Pa," bellowed Violet Katz, "there's a pink elephant outside my window!"

Mr. Katz was taking his morning bath. He blew the soapsuds into a bubble.

"Don't be so silly, Violet. It's too early in the morning for a joke."

"Well," said Violet Katz to herself, "if they don't want to believe me that's their bad luck."

And she got up and opened the window. The elephant put its pink trunk into her bedroom, picked her up and lifted her outside and onto its back.

Violet Katz gave an encouraging elephant call and they were off!

Mrs. Katz looked out of the kitchen window. She dropped the porridge spoon in surprise.

"Pa, Pa, come quick! Violet has just ridden off on the back of a large pink elephant."

Mr. Katz jumped out of his bath and rushed downstairs and out of the front door.

"Come back! Come back!" he called.

But Violet Katz and the pink elephant were far away in the distance.

A large policeman came round the corner.

"Help me, please," cried Mr. Katz. "My daughter's just ridden off on the back of a large pink elephant."

"Excuse me, sir," said the policeman, "but you haven't

got any clothes on and you're not allowed to walk round the streets like that."

Mr. Katz looked at himself. He thought quickly.

"I have got clothes on," he said. "They're made of a very new material – gossamer foam. Many uninformed people mistake them for soapsuds."

"Well, if I were you, sir, I'd go back and change them for something more conventional," remarked the policeman.

Mr. Katz went home.

"Did you find her?" asked Mrs. Katz tearfully.

"No, I did not," said Mr. Katz, "*and* I'm lucky I wasn't arrested. Now, as she's not here and she clearly won't be back for ages, I'm having her porridge as well as my own."

Meanwhile Violet Katz and the pink elephant were heading towards the ocean.

"Would you enjoy a day by the sea?" enquired the elephant.

"I'd love it," shouted Violet Katz, and she let go of the elephant's neck as she rode along. "Look, no hands!"

"I can do trunkstands," said the elephant proudly, and he lifted Violet down and set her on the ground. "Look at me."

"That's brilliant," said Violet, impressed.

"I know," said the elephant modestly. "That's why I'm pink. I'm always blushing with pride about how clever I am."

He put her up on his back again.

"I'm clever too," said Violet. "I can sing and whistle and dance."

"Remarkably smart," said the elephant. "Can you charge?"

"Well, no," admitted Violet, "I can't charge, but I am *extremely* good at throwing a tantrum."

"Really. I've never seen a tantrum. What is it?"

"It's a very bad fit of temper," explained Violet.

The elephant was curious.

"Could you throw one now?"

"Not now," said Violet. "I think I'll save it up for later just in case I need it."

They had been going for some time when suddenly the elephant said, "I can see the sea!"

"Where?"

"There, in front of us."

Violet Katz looked over the elephant's ear and saw way ahead in the distance the thin blue line of the ocean.

"Faster! Faster!" she cried.

The elephant's pink ears flapped out behind him as he raced along.

"Oh, Violet Katz," he called, "I love the sea."

They raced onto the soft brown sand, and sighed with pleasure at having arrived.

"Oh dear," said Violet, "I've just remembered. I haven't got a swimming costume. I'm still in my nightie."

The elephant looked thoughtful.

"I think we can work out something," he murmured.

"Well, what?" demanded Violet. "Here I am at the seaside in my nightie. People are going to stare at me and laugh."

"*I'm* not laughing."

"You don't count," said Violet very rudely.

The elephant was hurt.

"I'm not going to help you if you aren't kind to me," he said.

"I can't be kind when I'm worried," said Violet. "And I'm worried about not having proper clothes."

"All right," answered the elephant. "I've got an idea. I'll put you down in the sand and cover you up to your neck, and you can wait for me while I get some clothes for you."

He scooped up sand with his trunk and carefully buried her up to her neck.

"I'll be back soon," he told her.

And away he went.

Ten minutes later he was back with a beautiful frog green bathing suit and a bright red bath towel.

Violet put on the bathing suit.

"But where did you get them?"

"I borrowed them," explained the elephant.

"Who from?"

"From a clothesline I know. I promised to give them back later. And now that you're ready let's go for a swim!"

They raced each other into the water. Violet won because the elephant's big feet kept sinking into the wet sand.

They swam far out to sea. When Violet Katz got tired, the elephant lay on his back and she lay on his stomach.

"Do you get sunburnt?" she asked him.

"No," he replied. "When I've had too much sun I just go a very dark red."

He sucked up a trunkful of water and sprayed it into the air.

Then he bent his trunk the other way, and Violet climbed onto his head and slid down into the water. Splash!

"I think it's time to get out," remarked the elephant. "I don't know about you, but I'm getting hungry."

"Me too," agreed Violet.

They swam back to shore.

"There's a sandwich bar further down the beach and an icecream stand next door to it," said the elephant.

Violet put her hand in his trunk and they set off down the beach together.

They got to the sandwich bar and stood in the queue until it was their turn.

"I'm terribly hungry now," said Violet. "I'm going to have a cheese and tomato salad sandwich and an apple and some orange juice, and after that I'll have a big icecream."

"*I'm* going to have a hay and peanut butter sandwich and an apple and a bun and then a double size chocolate whopper icecream," said the elephant greedily. "Yum, yum. I'm starving."

Violet gave their orders to the man in the sandwich stall. He cut the bread and made the sandwiches. Then he wrapped everything up in paper bags.

"Here you are, Miss," he said. "That will be one pound and fifty eight pence."

"It's one pound and fifty eight pence," said Violet to the elephant. And she held out her hand for the money.

"I don't have any money," said the elephant. "I'm only an elephant. I thought you had some money."

"And I'm only a child. I don't have any money either. I thought *you* had some."

"I don't care which of you has the money as long as one of you pays me," said the man in the stall.

"We can't pay you. We don't have any money," explained Violet.

"Well, I can't afford to give them away," said the man. "Tell you what, I'll put them on one side and you can go and get the money and come back for them."

"Thank you," said Violet.

They went off together.

"I'm starving," said Violet. "I went off in such a hurry I didn't have my breakfast."

"I'm hungry, too," moaned the elephant. "Elephants have to eat such a lot to keep fit and I haven't had any breakfast today either."

"Didn't your mother give you any?" asked Violet.

" I don't have a mother," said the elephant sadly. "I ran away to join a circus when I was young and I quite lost contact with my family."

"Where do you live?" asked Violet.

"That's another thing," said the elephant gloomily. "I don't have a home of my own. I don't really belong anywhere. I was looking in your window this morning because it looked so nice inside your house and your bedroom looked so comfortable."

"It is quite nice," said Violet. "We don't have a car though because we can't afford it. And we don't have a television set either."

"What do you do in the evenings?"

"Well, in the evenings sometimes we go for a walk, sometimes my mother plays the harmonica to us or my father does acrobatic tricks, sometimes we have friends in to supper and sometimes we paint and colour in."

"It sounds wonderful," said the elephant wistfully. "Do you, by any chance, have a Christmas tree at Christmas?"

"Of course we do," cried Violet. "*And* we have coloured lights and presents on it."

"How lovely," said the elephant longingly.

"As a matter of fact, I'm getting hungrier every minute," Violet said, "and all this talk about home is making me even hungrier still. Shall we go home and get something?"

"I couldn't possibly take you home till I've had something to eat, I'm afraid."

"Well," said Violet, "we shall just have to earn some money somehow,"

"Maybe I could steal a bun with my trunk," said the elephant.

"You can't do that." Violet was definite. "It's not a good thing to do at all."

"Well, how will we make the money?"

"I'm considering," said Violet. "Ssh. Be quiet for a minute. I can't think if you're talking to me."

She sat down on the sand. Suddenly she jumped up.

"I've got it!" she cried. "You can give rides to the children for ten pence each. If you take three children each time, that will be thirty pence. And you'll only have to give six rides altogether."

"I don't really want to," said the elephant, "because I'm so tired. And anyway what are *you* going to do?"

"*I'm* going to do the publicity and the notices," said Violet.

"We haven't got any paper or chalk or anything to write on."

"We don't need it!" Violet said triumphantly. "We've got the whole beach. Look!"

And she took a stick and wrote in the sand

ELEPHANT RIDES.   10p PER CHILD

The elephant was doubtful.

"Supposing nobody comes."

"They will," said confident Violet.

"I'm tired," sighed the elephant.

"I know," answered Violet. "And as soon as you've done one ride for three children, I'll run down to the icecream stall and bring you back a chocolate whopper."

"All right," agreed the elephant. "I'll do it."

"Roll up, roll up," called Violet. "Elephant rides! Elephant rides! Only ten pence per child. Roll up, roll up." Then she turned to the elephant. "Try to look more relaxed," she whispered.

"I don't *feel* relaxed," muttered the elephant. "The thought of a lot of children clambering over me is very upsetting."

"Nonsense," said Violet briskly. "You'll love it. Besides, think what fun it will be for them."

A very old lady came up and peered at the notice in the sand.

"Elephant rides! How exciting," she cried. "How much are they for adults?"

"We don't take *adults*," said Violet.

"Whyever not?" The old lady was surprised. "I'd love an elephant ride. Would he take me for twenty pence? I'm not very heavy."

"For twenty pence I think he might," replied Violet. "I'll ask him."

"I will, I will, as long as it gets me my chocolate whopper soon," said the elephant.

He swung the old lady up in his trunk. She shrieked with excitement.

"Goodness me, it's just like the Big Wheel at the fair."

The elephant had just put her on his back when a very fat man appeared.

"Can I have a ride, please?" he asked.

"You're not a child, I'm afraid," said Violet.

"Oh dear," said the fat man. "We adults are always being discriminated against. Can I have a ride if I pay thirty pence? That's fair."

"Yes, it is," agreed Violet. "All right, you can."

The elephant sighed deeply, took a big breath and swung the fat man up on his back.

The fat man giggled.

"There's a wonderful view from up here," he called.

"Splendid, isn't it?" remarked the old lady.

"Marvellous!" said the fat man. "I haven't had an elephant ride since I was a boy."

Violet patted the elephant's trunk.

"We've got fifty pence already," she whispered. "You *are* doing well."

A man and a woman came up together. They looked exactly alike except that the man wore a striped shirt and trousers and the woman wore a striped blouse and skirt. They both wore identical straw hats and black shoes.

"Can you take us?" they said together.

"One," said Violet, "but not both. One of you will have to wait."

"But we must go together," they said in chorus. "We're twins. We do everything together all the time."

"Dear, dear," trumpeted the elephant. "I suppose I shall have to take them, but it's very bad for my back. And I'm quite worn out already."

Violet took a deep breath.

"He'll take you," she said, "but it will be fifty pence each."

"It's worth it," cried the twins at once.

The elephant curled his trunk round them both and lifted them up in the air.

"What fun," they shouted. "This *is* exciting."

"I'm ready to go," announced the elephant.

"Just a minute," said Violet, "there's something shining in the sand."

She reached down and picked it up. It was a ten pence piece!

"We've got one pound and sixty pence," she said proudly to the elephant. "I'll go and pay for the food and bring it back while you take them for their ride."

"Don't forget the icecream," reminded the elephant, and he lumbered off with everyone calling out eagerly on his back.

Violet set off for the sandwich stall.

"Here you are again," said the sandwich man. "Got your money now, have you?"

"Yes," said Violet. "Here it is. Thank you for keeping our sandwiches."

"Pleasure," remarked the man, and handed her the package.

Violet Katz set off back along the beach humming to herself. She had got halfway back when she suddenly had a terrible thought. She had spent all the money except two pence and she hadn't got any icecream!

"Oh dear!" she cried aghast. "I promised the elephant and I completely forgot and now I haven't got any money left."

And she sat down in the sun to think.

A boy came by with a double vanilla icecream cone.

"How much did that cost?" asked Violet.

"Twenty five pence," said the boy.

"Fifty pence for two," thought Violet, and aloud she said. "Would you like to see me stand on my head?"

"Oh yes," said the boy.

"It will cost you five pence," said Violet.

"I think my brother would like to see you too," said the boy. "I'll just go and get him."

Violet wrote a large notice in the sand.

PERFORMING GIRL.   HEADSTANDS,
ACROBATICS, DANCING AND WHISTLING.
5p PER PERSON.

A crowd began to collect.

"When does it start?" someone asked.

"As soon as we have ten or twelve people," explained Violet.

"There are fourteen people here already," said a man.

Violet collected the money. Seventy pence.

Another man came up and paid his five pence. Seventy five pence.

They made a circle round Violet and she began. She danced, she whistled, she tumbled and forward rolled and finally she stood on her head.

All the people clapped and cheered. Violet bowed.

"Thank you very much," she said and bowed again. Then she picked up her seventy five pence and made her way quickly to the icecream stall.

"Two double whoppers with chocolate sticks, please," she said to the man.

"Coming up," replied the man.

Violet took the icecreams and ran as fast as she could along the beach.

The elephant was sitting in the sand looking very sulky.

"I thought you were never coming back," he said crossly.

"Look," said Violet, "I've brought you a double chocolate whopper with a chocolate flake stick!"

The elephant shot out his trunk and seized the icecream.

"DELICIOUS!!!" he said. "I needed that. Thank you!"

He smiled at Violet.

"Let's have another swim," he said.

"After my lunch," Violet insisted. "I've got to eat."

"Swim first," said the elephant, "then eat."

So they splashed into the water and cooled off.

When they came out they ate their lunch.

"Oh," sighed Violet, "I feel *much* better."

The elephant yawned contentedly.

"There's *nothing* like a hay and peanut butter sandwich," he murmured.

They lay under a tree and went to sleep.

When they woke up it was still sunny. First they built a sandcastle and made a moat around it, then the elephant sucked up water in his trunk and filled the moat.

Suddenly, there was a shout from further down the beach and the old lady who had had the elephant ride came rushing up.

"Thank goodness!" she called. "I've been looking for you everywhere. I enjoyed the ride so much that I went home and emptied my money box and got out my tutu and I've come back for some more rides. I used to be in a circus when I was a girl and I want to see if I can still ride an elephant bare-back standing on one leg. Will you let me try?"

"Of course," said Violet and the elephant together.

The old lady tipped a pile of money onto the sand, gave Violet her bag to hold and went off to change. She came back in a beautiful pink and white tutu.

"It's very old," she said proudly, "but it still fits me."

She lifted her arms high into the air, the elephant wrapped his trunk round her waist and raised her up and onto his back. The old lady took a minute to get her balance, then, very slowly, she stood on her left toe and lifted her right leg high in the air behind her.

"Wonderful!" cried Violet.

The elephant moved slowly forward: the old lady went on balancing beautifully on his back.

All along the beach they went. People came running out of the water and dropped whatever they were doing to come and watch.

"Magnificent! Amazing! Fantastic!" cheered the people.

The old lady was overjoyed.

"I haven't had such a wonderful time for years," she cried. "Come home to tea with me."

So Violet and the elephant went to tea at the old lady's enormous and beautiful house. They sat on the lawn because the elephant couldn't get in through the front door.

When they had finished, Violet said, "I really think I must be getting home. Ma and Pa will be wondering where I am, and they'll be worried if I don't get back soon."

The elephant got up.

"Thank you for a delicious tea," he trumpeted.

The old lady waved goodbye and made them promise to visit if ever they were at the seaside again.

"And now," said the elephant, "home! But first I have to return those clothes, so you'd better get back into your nightie."

"I'd feel very silly in my nightie at five o'clock," objected Violet.

"Well, you can't wear nothing at all," the elephant pointed out. Then he suddenly had an idea.

"We've got lots of money from the old lady. We could go and buy you some new clothes and I could have a striped scarf. I've always wanted a striped scarf."

Violet was very pleased.

"What a wonderful idea!"

So off they went.

The man in the shop was rather surprised to see Violet in her nightie, but he sold her a new set of clothes and a striped scarf.

Violet put on her new trousers and T-shirt and asked

him to wrap up her nightgown, then she walked up the elephant's trunk and sat down on his back and they raced off home.

The elephant was very quiet on the way.

"What's the matter?" asked Violet.

"It's nothing," said the elephant. Then he said miserably, "Well, I may as well tell you, I wish *I* had a home to go back to."

"Where do you sleep at night?" asked Violet.

"Usually in a field, if it's warm, and in a barn or some sort of old building, if it's wet. But I'm always moving round. I'd like a *proper* home of my own," sighed the elephant.

"I think you'd better come home with me," said Violet.

"But what about your parents?" The elephant was anxious. "Maybe they won't want an elephant."

"Of course they'll want an elephant," Violet declared. "Why shouldn't they? Come on, let's go faster."

The elephant was going at a great pace. Soon they saw Violet's house ahead of them with Mr. Katz looking out of the window.

"Ma, Ma," yelled Mr. Katz. "come quickly. Violet has just ridden home on the back of a big RED elephant."

Mrs. Katz dropped her spoon in the home-brew mix.

"I don't believe it. You're seeing things, Pa."

"I am not. Just you look outside the front door."

At that moment the elephant poked his long red trunk through the window. Mrs. Katz screamed.

"Have you got a bun, Ma!" called Violet from the elephant's back.

Mrs. Katz took a wholemeal loaf from the cupboard and gave it to the elephant.

Violet slid down the elephant's trunk through the window and landed on the kitchen floor.

"Violet Katz," said her mother wearily, "this morning you rode off without telling us on the back of a large pink elephant and now you've come home on a big *red* one. What HAVE you been doing?"

"As a matter of fact," replied Violet, "I've been to the seaside for the day. And the elephant *was* pink but he went red in the sun."

"The seaside!" cried her parents together. "But it's *miles* away."

"I know. But elephants move quickly."

"And you went in your nightie!" said Mrs. Katz reproachfully.

"It's all your fault for not listening to me when I told you about the elephant. No one believed me," explained Violet. "And I went in my nightdress because I didn't have time to change. But just wait a minute."

She climbed back up the elephant's trunk, out through the window and onto his back, then slid down again carrying a bundle in her arms.

"Look!"

"What is it?" cried the Katzes.

"My nightie," said Violet proudly. "The elephant and I worked on the beach and earned the money for the new clothes I'm wearing. *And* here's a new bathing towel. And I've had lunch and been swimming and I've had a *lovely* day. Now where can we keep my elephant?"

"KEEP IT?" screamed Mr. Katz. "We can't keep an ELEPHANT."

"Why not?" asked Violet calmly.

"Because we can't, that's why."

"Well, it's him or me," said Violet. "Either he comes here or I go off with him."

"We couldn't bear to lose you," sighed her mother. "It was bad enough worrying about you today, so I suppose we'll have to keep the elephant. But where on earth can we put it?"

"We can't keep it," said Mr. Katz, "we're not allowed to have pets in this house."

"It's not a PET," said Violet scornfully. "How could anyone call it a pet? It's a vehicle. I've been riding on it all day."

"I suppose it *is* a vehicle," said Mr. Katz doubtfully.

"Of course he is." Violet was positive. "And if he had number plates he'd be definitely a vehicle."

"I do have a pair of number plates in the cupboard, as a matter of fact," said Mrs. Katz. "They're left over from my motorcycle. When I sold it, the woman who bought it wanted new ones with her initials on so I kept the old ones."

She got them out.

"But how will we hang them on the elephant?" asked Mr. Katz.

"Easy!" said Violet. "We put a string through the holes at each end and hang one over his tail and one over his trunk."

"Do you think we could go shopping on him?" asked Mrs. Katz.

"Yes, of course. And we could go to the seaside quite often," said Violet. "Now, where's he going to sleep?"

"That *is* a problem," said Mr. Katz. And he thought hard.

"There's a basement under the house," said Mrs. Katz. "I used to keep my motorbike in there."

"The door's too small," said Violet. "We couldn't get an elephant through a little door like that."

"What a pity," said Mr. Katz. "Because the basement would be perfect."

The pink elephant put his red trunk lovingly round

Violet's shoulder. She climbed out to scratch his ears.

"Can I stay?" he asked anxiously.

"We're just sorting out where you can sleep," explained Violet.

"I'm not fussy," said the elephant humbly. "Any old stable will do me."

"We don't actually have a stable," said Violet. "That's what the problem is. But don't worry. We'll solve it."

She clambered back inside.

They sat round the table, still thinking. Suddenly Mrs. Katz thumped the table hard and jumped to her feet.

"I have it! The perfect answer!"

"What? What?" cried Violet and her father.

"Just wait a minute," said Mrs. Katz mysteriously.

She went out of the room and was back two minutes later with her tool kit.

"If we can't get Violet's elephant in through the basement door, we'll have to get him in through the basement roof."

"But the basement is under the house. The basement roof is just below the kitchen floor." Mr. Katz was puzzled.

"Exactly," said Mrs. Katz. "I am now going to make the kitchen floor into a trapdoor and we can put a ramp down into the basement for Violet's elephant."

"It's a wonderful idea," said Mr. Katz slowly, "but how do we get the elephant through the front door of the house?"

"Easy!" shouted Mrs. Katz. "Simple! We take out the

bay windows and put them back in afterwards, and tomorrow I shall knock out the small basement door and build a big sliding up-and-over door so the elephant can get in and out easily. But at least tonight he won't have to sleep outside in the cold."

Violet took a hammer, Mrs. Katz took a crowbar, Mr. Katz took a saw, the elephant took some nails, and they started work.

In no time at all they had turned the kitchen floor into a trap door.

In a very short time they had made a ramp. And finally they took out the windows.

And then, with a lot of pushing and pulling and to-ing and fro-ing, they finally got the elephant through the gap inside the house. Mr. Katz lifted the trap door, and the elephant walked down the ramp and into his basement.

"How delightful," he trumpeted happily. "A place of my own at last."

Mr. and Mrs. Katz and Violet put the windows back in place and put the tools away.

"And now," said Mr. Katz, "it's suppertime."

"Oh good," said the elephant eagerly. "What's for supper?"

Mr. and Mrs. Katz and Violet looked at one another.

"Oh dear!" said Violet. "I forgot about his food."

"What does he eat?" asked Mrs. Katz.

Violet looked worried. "Hay and stale buns and occasionally peanuts."

They sat down to think hard again.

Suddenly Mr. Katz jumped up and banged on the table.

"I've got it! I've got it," he shouted.

"What? What?" cried Mrs. Katz and Violet.

"Why, it's simple," said Mr. Katz happily. "Every Thursday, the elephant can do free deliveries for the bakery, and in return they can give him all their stale buns every night. And the hay's no problem at all. Hay is just dried grass. Violet and her elephant can collect the grass cuttings once a week from the park."

"You're a very clever person," said Mrs. Katz admiringly.

"But meantime, what do we feed him tonight?" asked Violet.

"Scones and crumpets of course," said Mrs. Katz. "Your father was just going to bake some when you came in."

"So I was," said Mr. Katz. "How forgetful of me."

And he leaned down into the basement and called to the elephant.

"With or without cheese?"

"What?" enquired the elephant.

"Your scones," replied Mr. Katz.

"Oh, with, please," answered the elephant.

Mr. Katz put on his apron. Mrs. Katz swept up the woodshavings.

They looked at Violet.

"Ma," said Mr. Katz, "I think we're very lucky to have an interesting daughter like Violet."

"Pa," said Mrs. Katz, "I think I agree with you."

Violet smiled at them both.

And down in the basement Violet's pink elephant trumpeted happily in his new home.

THE GREBBLE
and the
FLOOD

The grebble and Arsinoee
Did everything they could
To live together happily
But things were not so good.

They realised the problem was
Her house was very small,
They both were squashed: they couldn't move,
There was no space at all.

And, once again, the two of them
Had spent a sleepless night.
The grebble found it very cramped.
(The fit was rather tight.)

"I'll leave my tail outside the house,"
The grebble kindly said.
"And also," said Arsinoee,
"You'd better leave your head."

"Oh dear!" the grebble cried, "I know
I can't stay in this place."
"What nonsense!" said Arsinoee,
"We'll simply make more space."

She set off to the village store
But everywhere she walked,
The village people looked away
And no one smiled or talked.

She bought some nails; she bought some wood,
She went to get a saw.
The villagers were gathered
In a group outside the door.

"Arsinoee," said Dr. Brown,
"We've got to have a word.
You cannot keep the grebble here.
The idea's quite absurd.

We're grateful. You're a clever child.
You saved us all, we know.
But that's a very dangerous beast.
Your grebble has to go."

"I'm sorry," said Arsinoee,
And firmly set her jaw,
"The grebble stays and lives with me.
I'm saying nothing more."

"It's dangerous," the doctor said,
"There isn't any doubt.
And if you won't co-operate,
We're going to drive it out."

Arsinoee was very cross.
Her eyes went brightest pink.
"You'd better watch your step," she said.
"I'm going off to THINK."

And, as she walked and tried to think
Of what to do, she saw
The grebble creeping down the road,
A suitcase in its claw.

"Oh Grebble," asked Arsinoee,
"What are you going to do?"
"I'm leaving," sobbed the grebble,
"So they won't be cross with you."

"You mustn't!" said Arsinoee.
"You're staying here with me.
I'll work it out and find a plan.
Don't cry. Just wait and see."

They had their supper, went to bed,
And, sometime in the night,
A storm began with pouring rain.
They woke up in a fright.

"My tail's all wet!" the grebble cried.
"There's water all around.
It's raining hard: it's lashing down:
There're puddles on the ground."

The morning came: the sun shone down,
But everything in Swipping
The houses, people, cats and dogs
Was flooded out and dripping.

Arsinoee was greatly pleased.
"Get up, sweet beast," she said.
"The answer to our problem's come
While we were both in bed."

"Arsinoee," the grebble said,
"I really can't see how."
"They need your breath," the girl replied,
"To dry the village now.

You'll have to breathe out fire and smoke
And really look ferocious."
The grebble said, "You told me
Such behaviour was atrocious.

I *used* to be a wicked beast
But now I'm very good.
I'd like to use my fire to help
But I don't think I could."

Arsinoee was quite annoyed.
She hit the grebble's head.
"Watch out!" she cried. "I'm going to take
Away your jam and bread."

The grebble gave a mighty roar.
It shot out flames and heat
And dried the raging torrent up
That poured along the street.

The steam rose up. The grebble
Gave the door a mighty slam,
And, breathing fire, set off at once
In search of bread and jam.

Arsinoee was very quick.
She snatched up jam and bread
And crept along unnoticed
With the grebble just ahead.

The villagers were standing round
In rubber boots and macs.
They'd tried to keep the water out
By putting sand in sacks.

Alas! It simply hadn't worked:
The rains had been too strong.
The sacks had burst: the water
Through the streets had spread along.

"What can we do?" the people asked
And some began to cry.
"Our houses, clothes and shops are soaked!
We'll never get things dry."

Just then they heard a splashing sound
And slowly, looking mean,
The grebble through the water came
Towards the village green.

"I want some bread and jam!" it shrieked.
"I WANT SOME JAM AND BREAD!"
Behind it swam Arsinoee
A bag perched on her head.

THE GREBBLE AND THE FLOOD

The grebble blew out tongues of flame
And gave a frightening scream.
The water in the village street
Dried up and turned to steam.

"Oh look!" the people called, amazed.
"The water's almost dried.
Bring out the clothes and mattresses
And everything inside."

They hung things from the windowsills
And hauled the rest outside
And every time the grebble roared
A little more got dried.

Arsinoee had slipped upstairs
And held the jam and bread
Just out of reach but well in view
Above the grebble's head.

The grebble turned towards the food,
Its tail swung swiftly round
And swept away the dried-up mud
That lay along the ground

"Arsinoee!" the grebble roared.
"I thought you were my friend."
"I am," she sighed. "I'm helping you.
You'll see that in the end."

"If you're my friend," the grebble asked,
"Why won't you give me food?"
"I would have," said Arsinoee,
"But you were very rude.

You slammed the door and lumbered off.
You didn't wait to see.
But, even so, I'm still your friend,
I've brought your food with me."

The monster blushed a purple-pink
And sadly hung its head.
"Arsinoee, I just forgot,
I'm sorry now," it said.

And suddenly, behind them, came
The noise of many feet.
The people, bringing presents, rushed
Along the village street.

"You've got to stay! We need you here!
We'll fix your house!" they cried.
"You're now a local hero here!"
Arsinoee grinned wide.

The villagers set off with wood
And hammers, nails and saws.
They raised the roof, enlarged the walls,
And put in bigger doors.

THE GREBBLE AND THE FLOOD

"It's wonderful," the grebble said,
"To know they all want me.
I couldn't bear to live alone
Without Arsinoee."

Arsinoee looked very smart.
"I said you needn't fear.
I *knew* that what we needed
Was a grebble living here.

Now thanks a lot and home you go.
It's late and getting dark.
You needn't fear. *We're* looking after
Swipping-on-the-Nark."

GEORGIANA
and the
DRAGON

Once upon a time in a far country, there lived a king in a golden palace. The palace had television in every room, a soda fountain in the billiard room, and in the throne room an icecream making machine which could produce one hundred and forty-seven different flavoured icecreams. All the waterfalls in the palace gardens were made of lemonade, and the mud at the edges was chocolate.

The king had one child, his daughter, the Princess Georgiana. She had red hair and green eyes, and a very hot temper, and she loved playing football and doing daring unusual things, whenever she could find any to do.

The king should have been very happy, but he had one serious problem. His kingdom was being terrorised by a huge dragon which had suddenly flown in a year before and had settled in a cave on the top of a hill thirteen miles from the palace. The king knew the cave very well indeed because he had had a treasure hoard hidden there just in case he should ever need it, and now the dragon was in the cave guarding the treasure and making it impossible for the king to get it back.

"The whole situation's hopeless," sighed the king to his Lord Chamberlain.

"It does seem so, Your Majesty," agreed the Lord Chamberlain.

"And," went on the king tragically, "as if that's not bad enough, the wretched beast has taken to going out from time to time and breathing on the crops and forests and burning them up. Three of the peasants have lost their houses as well. Everybody's getting very fed up and they're all expecting *me* to do something about it."

"Well, you *are* the king, after all. It's only natural they should look to you for help," murmured the respectful Lord Chamberlain.

"I don't see that at all." The king was belligerent. "It's certainly my bad luck but that doesn't make it my responsibility."

The Lord Chamberlain was firm.

"Well, the people see it that way, Your Majesty. And if Your Majesty wants to keep their loyalty and support, and remain a much-loved monarch . . ."

"All right, all right," muttered the king. "So what should I do about it?"

"With respect . . ." began the Lord Chamberlain.

"Forget the respect," said the king testily. "And get on with the ideas. And quickly."

The Lord Chamberlain quietly ground his teeth together and went on.

"As I was saying, what Your Majesty needs is a contest."

"A contest?"

"To find a young prince to kill the dragon and free the people from their worries about it and the bonfires it creates, and also to release Your Majesty's treasure."

"It's a good idea in theory," said the king, "but in practice, I can't think of any princes, or even knights, come to that, who'd be crazy enough to do it. That dragon breathes fire."

"Exactly," said the Lord Chamberlain, "which is why Your Majesty is offering a large reward. It's called an incentive," he explained.

"But I'm not offering one," said the king, puzzled.

"You must, Your Majesty," replied the Lord Chamberlain. "Or none of them will agree to try."

"What shall I offer?" asked the king.

"In these cases," said the Lord Chamberlain, "it's usual to offer the hand of the Princess in marriage and half your kingdom."

"HALF MY KINGDOM!" The king was outraged. "That's insane."

"But necessary," assured the Lord Chamberlain.

"A quarter then," said the king sulkily.

"No, a quarter's too little," said the Lord Chamberlain. "Perhaps a third now and the rest when Your Majesty is no longer with us. Which, of course, we hope will not be for many, many years yet," he added hastily, noticing the king's expression.

"Well, as you say I've got no choice," said the king, "I'll

obviously have to do it. But I don't like it, I can tell you."

"Since Your Majesty's mind is now made up, I'll go off and draw up a set of rules for the contest and broadcast the news of the competition," said the Lord Chamberlain.

And he rushed off hastily before the king could change his mind.

The king went moodily over to the icecream machine and ordered himself a treble bubblegum, wild strawberry and Chinese king prawn icecream with a giant flake. Some time later, as he was finishing it, the Lord Chamberlain came back.

"I've drawn up the rules," he announced, "and I've posted notices of the contest all over the palace, and sent messengers off to all four corners of the kingdom to put up notices and spread the word."

"How long will that take?" asked the king.

"About an hour or two," said the Lord Chamberlain. "Three, at most. They all went on trail bikes."

By nightfall, fourteen knights and three princes had registered as contestants.

"I wish there were more princes," sighed the king.

"There might be. More may apply tomorrow," pointed out the Lord Chamberlain. "But I must remind Your Majesty that princes are in short supply. Really, I'm surprised that as many as three have entered."

"Prince Blanziflor's on the register, I see," said the king. "I'm pleased about that. His mother's an old friend of mine. I think he should try first. If I have to give up some of my kingdom, I don't mind so much if it's Blanziflor who wins it."

"He has to slay the dragon first," murmured the Lord Chamberlain.

In the next morning's mail bag there were another five applications.

"Superb," said the king. "We shall start tomorrow."

And he ordered a large canopy to be put up and invited all the people to watch a display by the princes and knights before they set off.

"They can stay in the palace until it's their own turn," he explained to the Lord Chamberlain and the Court Jester, "and we will have entertainments every night for them."

The jester hurried away looking pleased. He liked showing off at entertainments.

The following afternoon the dragon slayers assembled on their horses in the palace yard. From under the canopy a large crowd watched them, impressed. In the special royal box in the centre sat the Princess Georgiana and behind her sat the rest of the palace staff. The princess looked interestedly at the competitors.

"I hope the dragon gets them all," she remarked to the Lord Chamberlain.

"Your Highness!" The Lord Chamberlain was shocked.

"Well, I don't want to marry any of *them*," said the princess. "I don't even think much of their horses."

There was a scuffle at the portcullis. It was raised. The king peered out.

"Who is it?"

"It's me," gasped a voice, and in on a large white horse rode a rather scruffy looking prince in a football shirt.

"Prince Blanziflor, Your Majesty," he announced to the king, jumping off his horse and bowing low. A large guitar case was strapped on the back of his saddle.

"I got lost," he explained. "I'm sorry I'm late."

"You're just in time," said the king. "I know your mother. How is she?"

"Rather upset, I'm afraid," said Blanziflor. "She's very

worried that I'll be eaten by the dragon. I *am* her only son, you see. But, on the other hand, times are hard and there aren't many other kingdoms going begging at present, and it did seem a good opportunity . . ."

"Quite," said the king. "Naturally. Of course. Well," he went on, ushering Prince Blanziflor into the courtyard, "you're here now, and that's what counts."

"I say," said Prince Blanziflor, looking up. "Is that the princess? She looks rather nice." And he waved.

The Princess Georgiana waved back.

"Who's that?" she asked the Lord Chamberlain.

"Prince Blanziflor, I think," said the Lord Chamberlain.

"I hope the dragon doesn't eat *him*," said the princess thoughtfully.

The dragon-slayers' pageant began. The crowds cheered and applauded as the young princes and knights rode up and down the courtyard in their armour. When it was finally over, the king lit the bonfire for the royal fireworks display. The Princess Georgiana was watching the Catheine wheels and rockets when she felt a tap on her shoulder. She turned around.

"I say," said an eager voice, "I've been trying to meet you for ages. Hello."

"Hello!" said the princess. "Who are you?"

"I'm Prince Blanziflor."

"I'm the Princess Georgiana."

"I know," said the prince. "You look as if you're good fun. Can you play football?"

"I love it!" cried the princess. "If you sneak round the back with me we could kick a few balls secretly now whilst no one's looking."

"Oh yes!" said the prince.

He took her hand and together they crept away from the crowd and out onto the palace football pitch. They had been practising goals for quite some time when the princess said suddenly,

"What time is it?"

"I don't know," answered the prince. "I haven't got a watch. But it's quite late."

"Oh dear," said the Princess Georgiana, "I'm supposed to be at the banquet."

"So am I!" said the prince.

"But I'm the guest of honour."

"Well," said Blanziflor, "we'll just have to go in together and hope no one notices."

They went back to the palace entrance and slipped into the banqueting hall. The king looked up from the end of the golden table.

"Where have *you* been?" he said severely to his daughter.

"Oh, Papa . . ." began the princess, but Prince Blanziflor said loudly, "I'm terribly sorry, Your Majesty, I asked your daughter to show me the palace maze and I'm afraid we got lost."

"You seem to make a habit of getting lost," remarked the king. "Well, now that you both *are* here, you'd better sit down and start eating."

The Princess Georgiana sat on her father's right hand. Prince Blanziflor sat near the bottom of the table.

At the end of the meal the king rose and gave a speech of welcome and thanks to all the competitors. Then he announced, "The Lord Chamberlain has drawn lots to see who will have the first chance of meeting the dragon, and here is the list of princes and knights in the order they will go off to fight.

First, Prince Belvedere.

Second, the Star Green Knight.

Third . . ."

He droned on until the princess heard,

"Seventeenth, Prince Blanziflor."

"Maybe, by then," she thought, "the dragon will be badly wounded and Prince Blanziflor will succeed."

The banquet finished, and after drinking one another's health, everyone retired to bed.

The next day, to the accompaniment of great cheers, Prince Belvedere set off to fight the dragon.

The king's messenger returned the day after with unhappy news.

"I'm afraid, Sire, Prince Belvedere has perished."

In quick succession followed four knights and two more princes.

"Your Majesty," said the Lord Chamberlain, several days later, after the palace messenger had reported the sixteenth competitor frizzled up by dragon's breath or fatally wounded by dragon's claws, "is it sensible to continue?"

"As I recall," said the king, "this was *your* idea, not mine, so it's on your head, I'm afraid."

"The next contestant," announced the court usher, "has come to say farewell, Your Majesty. Prince Blanziflor."

The prince came jauntily into the throne room and sank on one knee.

"Your blessing, Sire," he murmured humbly.

"Good luck, my boy," said the king kindly. "And I hope you get my treasure back."

"And may I have *your* blessing, Your Highness," said Prince Blanziflor, bending low in front of the Princess Georgiana.

"Granted," replied the princess graciously. "And I have a piece of advice for you."

And she whispered in his ear, "If in doubt, give in and run."

Prince Blanziflor bowed and left.

Twelve hours later the king's messenger reappeared.

"Terrible news, Your Majesty. Prince Blanziflor has been taken prisoner by the dragon. He is being held hostage in the dragon's cave."

"How shocking!" cried the king. "We must send another contestant to rescue him."

"Impossible!" said the Lord Chamberlain. "There were only five more competitors, and they've all resigned. There's no one left to rescue him. You will have to go yourself, Sire."

"I'd love to go, of course," said the king, "but, unfortunately, I'm too old."

"Well, I don't know what we can do, Sire," said the Lord Chamberlain.

"His mother will be awfully cross," said the king thoughtfully.

"Undoubtedly, Sire."

"Are you sure there are no more contestants?"

"None at all, Sire," the Lord Chamberlain assured him.

They sat together for some time, thinking deeply.

The door opened and the Princess Georgiana came in.

"Yes, my dear?" asked the king.

"I've come to register," said the princess.

"Register?" The king was puzzled.

"For the contest."

The king looked even more puzzled. "What contest?"

"Really, Papa!" sighed the princess. "You *are* impossible. The dragon slaying contest, of course. I want to kill
the dragon."

"Georgiana!" cried the king. "Don't be so ridiculous.
You can't possibly kill the dragon. I've never heard such
nonsense."

"I *can* kill the dragon," said the princess calmly. "*And*
rescue Prince Blanziflor. And I've come to register. Can
you put my name down, please?" she asked, turning to the
Lord Chamberlain. "I want to be a contestant."

"Well, you can't," said the king firmly. "It has to be a
prince who slays the dragon."

"It doesn't say so in the rules," objected the princess.

"It does," said the Lord Chamberlain.

"Where, then?" demanded the princess.

The Lord Chamberlain took up the parchment scroll. He
read it through very thoroughly, then re-read it. He was on
the third re-read when the king said, nastily, "Well, come
on, read it aloud."

The Lord Chamberlain cleared his throat.

"I can't actually find it, Your Majesty."

"See!" said the princess triumphantly.

The king looked hard at the Lord Chamberlain.

"What do you mean, you can't find it? I thought it was
rule fifty-three."

"With respect, Your Majesty," mumbled the Lord Chamberlain, "rule fifty-three is to do with claims of compensation in the event of death by dragon's breath."

"I told you it wasn't in the rules," said the princess, "so I'm going."

"It's unfeminine," said the king. "No one's ever heard of a princess fighting a dragon."

"They will have after I've done it," said the princess.

The king sighed heavily.

"I wonder if commoners have these troubles," he remarked to the ceiling.

"Undoubtedly, Sire," cried the Lord Chamberlain and the Court Jester simultaneously.

"Not much consolation," said the king.

And to the princess he said, "Well, under the circumstances I don't suppose I can stop you."

"I'll need a longbow, this list of equipment and a red suit of armour," said the princess. "Do you think someone could get them for me by morning, please? Oh, and a banner, of course."

"I'll see to it myself," said the Lord Chamberlain, and he hurried away.

"Georgiana," said the king, "let me explain it to you once more. That dragon is ferocious and desperate. It's guarding a priceless treasure and it will stop at nothing to keep it. It has Prince Blanziflor imprisoned at the back of its cave; it's already sizzled up some of the knights and princes and frightened off the rest of them. This is a doomed enterprise."

"I'm going and that's that," said the princess in an even more determined tone.

The king looked resigned.

"I've tried to stop you," he said. "I've explained the dangers and, of course, you *are* my only daughter and I love you dearly, but if you won't listen to reason and you want to upset me and cause me grief and woe, go right ahead."

"That's emotional blackmail, Papa," said the Princess Georgiana. "You should be ashamed of yourself. And there won't be any grief or woe: you'll be rejoicing because the dragon's slain."

"Nobody's going to slay that dragon," answered the king. "How can they? It's impossible."

"I don't think so," said Georgiana, and then, with a sudden surge of enthusiasm, she asked, "Do you think, as it might be my last meal for ages, we could have passion-fruit layer cake for supper?"

"It might be your last meal ever, so I suppose we'd better," said the king moodily. "Order it from Cook. But I won't enjoy it much, I can tell you."

Princess Georgiana set off for the kitchen. On the way she met the Lord Chamberlain.

"Your Highness," began the Lord Chamberlain.

"Yes?"

"It's about your heraldic emblem. What creature would you like emblazoned on your shield? All the knights have an animal or bird or heraldic beast of some kind."

The princess thought for a bit. Then she said, "A gerbil, I think. I like gerbils."

"I'm not really sure that a gerbil is quite suitable," said the Lord Chamberlain.

"Well, it's what I want," answered the princess cheerily and she sped away to the kitchen.

The princess got up next morning, dressed in her new red armour which the maid had laid out ready for her, and went down to breakfast. Crowds of people were assembling outside the palace to watch her set off. She collected her equipment and her sandwiches, brushed her teeth thoroughly with her golden toothbrush, kissed the king and went outside.

The people cheered loudly and she gave a gracious wave as she jumped into her red sports car with the golden gerbil emblem on each door and the small gold crown on top, and set off. Behind her came a groom driving the royal horse-box with her horse, Bucephalus, inside.

About two miles from the dragon's cave the princess pulled up. The horse-box stopped behind her and the groom got out.

"You can get the horse ready now," said the princess carelessly. "I can see smoke on the horizon. It must be the dragon."

"I expect so, Your Highness," said the groom nervously, and he began to open the horse-box. He paused. "Your horse may not like the smoke," he pointed out.

"Bucephalus isn't frightened of *anything*. I trained him myself."

"Will Your Highness actually be needing me," asked the groom, "or will it be all right for me to go back to the palace?"

"Oh, you can go back," the princess assured him. "I can manage quite well by myself."

The groom saluted nervously. He set up the mounting steps. "Thank you, ma'am," he said with relief.

And he tied Bucephalus to a nearby tree, shut up the royal horse-box and jumped in behind the steering wheel.

Two seconds later he was out again. "Good luck, Your Highness."

"Oh thanks," said the princess and she waved to him as he drove away.

Bucephalus whinnied and lifted his head. The Princess Georgiana stroked his neck.

"Good boy," she said soothingly, and she untied the reins, climbed onto the mobile steps (because she was quite heavy in her armour) and got onto his back.

"Here we go," said the Princess Georgiana, and they set off to meet the dragon.

They had not gone far when the smoke began to get thicker and the air felt warmer.

"Thank goodness I had special heatproof armour made," thought the princess.

They rode on. As they approached the hill where the

dragon was guarding the cave, they could hear the sounds of a guitar.

"It must be Prince Blanziflor at the back of the cave. I expect that's how he passes the time," said the princess.

Bucephalus snorted.

Flames were shooting out of the cave entrance. The Princess Georgiana smiled to herself and thought contentedly of the fire extinguisher strapped to her sword case.

At the bottom of the hill she stopped, jumped down from Bucephalus's back and tied him to a large rock.

"Wait there like a good horse," she told him kindly, and patted his nose.

Bucephalus nuzzled her.

Princess Georgiana set off on foot up the hill to meet the dragon.

There was a rumble and a roar! The ground shook. Out of the cave poked a huge dragon's head.

"What do you want," it growled nastily.

The Princess smiled. "I've come sightseeing," she answered.

"Sightseeing!" snarled the dragon. "What do you mean? Sightseeing."

"I've come to see the dragon."

"I *am* the dragon," said the dragon proudly. "I terrorise the neighbourhood round here. I've frizzled up princes and knights with my hot breath already, and I've got a prince trapped in my cave. As a matter of fact," it went on confidentially, "I'm guarding a priceless treasure in there."

117

"You're not!" The Princess Georgiana was disbelieving.

"Oh yes, I am," said the dragon, and it spat nastily at her. A long flame shot out of its mouth.

"Could you do that again, please?" asked the princess.

"Why?"

"I just wondered if you could."

"Of course I can," said the dragon boastfully, and it shot out another sheet of flame.

"How nice," said the princess. She undid her quiver and took out a long toasting fork and a bag of marshmallows.

"Now, I'll just sit here with my fork and toast marshmallows on your breath, if you don't mind."

"Well, I'm not actually doing anything special right now, so I suppose I could," agreed the dragon.

They sat there for some time while the princess toasted and ate marshmallows.

"I don't believe you've really got a prince in there," said Princess Georgiana.

"I have." The dragon was confident.

"Well, where is he then?"

"I don't let him *out*," said the dragon scornfully. "He might run away. He's my hostage. He's playing the guitar in there now."

"I see," said the princess. "Where exactly have you put him?"

"He's right at the back of the cave."

"Oh."

She took another marshmallow from her bag, pushed it onto her fork and held it in front of the dragon.

"Blow again, please."

The dragon was irritated. "Look here," it rumbled. "I've got better things to do all day than sit about toasting things for silly girls."

"I'm not a silly girl," said the Princess Georgiana. "I'm actually very clever and strong *and* I can tap-dance."

"In full armour? I don't believe it," said the dragon.

"Of course, I can't tap-dance in my *armour*."

"And come to that," went on the dragon, "what are you doing in full armour anyway? Whoever heard of anyone sightseeing in armour."

The Princess Georgiana thought quickly. "Well, I am," she said, "so now you have heard of somebody doing it. My mother makes me wear it. I've got a very weak chest and she thinks it will stop me from catching cold."

"She sounds a bit over-protective," commented the dragon.

"She is," said the princess hastily. "But, of course, I have to do as she says."

"Quite right too," answered the dragon. "People should do as their mothers tell them."

"Do *you*?" The princess was curious.

"Of course not," said the dragon. "I'm a *dragon*. Dragons don't do as they're told."

The princess was thoughtful. "I see." Then she went on suddenly, "So it wouldn't be any use telling you to stay in that cave and not follow me to see what I'm doing when I go off in a few minutes."

"No, it would not," said the dragon. "Because I'll just follow you if I want to."

"What if I *ordered* you not to follow me?"

"I don't get ordered round by anyone, especially not girls. I'd just follow you anyway. You couldn't stop me."

"I see."

Princess Georgiana was thoughtful. She put another marshmallow on the fork, then quickly pulled it off and ate it untoasted.

"It's a pretty day," she remarked.

"Very," agreed the dragon.

They sat in companionable silence for some time.

"I expect your cave's rather dismal and ugly inside," said the princess.

The dragon was hurt. "It's actually very well decorated," it snapped. "And there's a beautiful gem collection in one corner."

The princess knew all about the gem collection: she had heard her father lamenting its loss frequently.

"Oh, really," she answered politely.

"You don't sound very impressed," complained the dragon.

"I'm sure your gems are very beautiful," replied the princess, "but I don't believe you've got as many as you say. I think you're boasting."

The dragon was furious. It roared out a cloud of black smoke and stamped till the ground rumbled.

The guitar music inside the cave stopped.

"How dare you?" shouted the dragon. "You ignorant girl. I'll show you if I'm boasting or not. Come inside and have a look and see if I'm telling the truth. You owe me a big apology."

"If it's true, I'll apologise," said the princess. "And if it's not true, you have to."

"IT IS TRUE!" screamed the dragon. "Go in there and look!"

It moved to one side of the cave entrance.

The princess went cautiously forward. It was very gloomy inside. She took a deep breath and stepped past the dragon, into the dark.

At first she could see nothing at all, then, as her eyes adjusted to the gloom, she noticed a faint glow at the very back of the cave. She moved towards it. As she drew nearer, she realised the glow came from an enormous heap of coloured stones.

"My goodness," breathed the princess to herself, "it must be the gem collection! But it can't be. It's enormous."

She looked hard. Diamonds, rubies, emeralds, sapphires, turquoises, opals and bars of gold and silver sparkled and gave off a soft warm light.

"Amazing!" sighed the princess aloud.

"I know," whispered a voice beside her.

"Prince Blanziflor!" said the princess.

She had forgotten all about him in the excitement of going into the dark cave.

"Ssh, quietly," he hissed. "The dragon has super-acute hearing. Don't let it hear you talking to me. I *am* Prince Blanziflor and I've been trapped here for ages. Can you get someone to free me?"

"I've come to free you," whispered Princess Georgiana.

"Good Heavens, it's Princess Georgiana! You free me?" The prince stifled a giggle. "Why, you're a girl!"

"I'm a princess actually," said Georgiana huffily, "and if you don't want to be rescued that's fine with me. Just let me know and I'll leave straightaway."

"Oh no, please." The prince was humble. "I'm sorry. I don't care who rescues me, as long as I get out of here. I can only play three tunes on the guitar and I'm sick to death of them, and all that dragon gives me to eat is porridge. Can you imagine it?" he went on gloomily. "Porridge, porridge, porridge, three times a day. It's awful."

"You're lucky the dragon hasn't killed you," said the princess. "Why doesn't it?"

"It thinks I'm too useful as a hostage," explained the prince. "But I don't see how you're going to rescue me. There's no chance. It's killed the others already."

"I know," said the princess. "I say, I think I might just slip a diamond in my quiver and take it with me."

"Don't, don't!" Prince Blanziflor was very agitated. "You mustn't. The last time that happened it burnt up the knight who did it in one breath. Just like a flame-thrower. It was terrible."

"How awful!" whispered the princess. "But it won't know I've taken it."

"It will. It'll smell it," explained the prince.

"Smell it?"

"Yes. Dragons can smell precious stones: their noses are very sensitive to gems and they can smell diamonds and rubies over fifty metres away."

"Gosh!" The princess was impressed.

"That's how it found this treasure," went on Prince Blanziflor. "It was flying by and it smelt it and burned down the huge wooden doors at the cave entrance with its fiery breath and it's been here ever since, guarding it."

"I see," said the princess. "Well, I won't take one now I know that." She thought for a minute. "I'd better go out soon or it'll get suspicious. And I've got a plan. If you want to be rescued you'll have to do as I say." And she whispered urgently in his ear.

"Yes, I will," muttered Prince Blanziflor. "But do be careful, won't you?"

"No," said the princess. "I won't be careful: I'll be clever. See you later. And don't forget to do exactly what I told you."

"Goodbye," said Prince Blanziflor.

The princess went out of the cave and stood blinking in the sunlight by the entrance.

The dragon looked at her and took a deep breath.

"You didn't take anything," it said in astonishment.

"Of course not," answered Princess Georgiana. "*I'm* not a thief. And I owe you an apology. That's a WONDERFUL collection of jewels – the best I've ever seen."

The dragon looked proud.

"Where did you get them?"

"I found them," it said arrogantly. "All by myself. I smelt them as I was flying by."

"But didn't they belong to someone else?"

"They're mine now," remarked the dragon.

"But that's stealing."

The dragon was enraged.

"Shut up, shut up!" it shouted. "I won't listen. Stop accusing me." And it stamped and screamed. The ground rumbled.

"Honestly, you are a baby," said the princess, unimpressed. "Do stop it. You're making earthquakes. And I want to tell you something. You've got someone in that cave, did you know?"

"Of course I know, I told you already. It's a prince. He's my hostage."

"Oh yes, so you did," replied the princess. "What do you feed him?"

"Porridge," explained the dragon. "It's very good for him."

"Porridge!" The princess was incredulous. "Seriously?"

"Yes. Why not?" the dragon was puzzled.

"Well, no reason why not," said the Princess Georgiana, "except I personally wouldn't waste good porridge on a hostage."

"What do you mean?"

"It seems to me," said the princess slowly, "that it's a terrible waste of a precious food to give porridge to a *hostage*. I wouldn't. But I suppose you can afford it with a gem collection like yours."

"I can't, I can't. I'm terribly poor, actually," moaned the dragon. "It's dreadful. I haven't *any* money at all. And I can't sell my treasure. I thought he didn't like porridge and it served him right to be made to eat it."

"Well, have it your own way, then. I don't care," answered the princess.

"How do you mean? You must tell me. What should I feed him?"

"You can do as you want," said the princess, "but if I, personally, had a hostage like that, I certainly wouldn't waste valuable porridge on him. I'd make him eat bacon and eggs every morning, and baked beans and ham and sausages and tomatoes and roast potatoes and horrible things like that."

"But I thought he would *like* those sorts of things. I want to make life hard for him."

The princess threw back her head and laughed and laughed.

"You are silly," she cried. "Fancy punishing someone by feeding him porridge. Have it your own way. Carry on, but I'll bet he loves porridge just like I do."

"Right!" said the dragon grimly. "No more porridge for him! From now on he gets bacon and eggs and baked beans."

"Whatever you do, don't give him water either," said the princess. "Make him drink lemonade or something sickly and gassy like that."

"All right," said the dragon. "And thank you. You are a help."

"I try to be," said the Princess Georgiana. "And if I were you, I'd start with the baked beans now. Just watch his face when you give them to him. He'll be really upset."

"Yes, I will," said the dragon.

"Well, I'll be off to do some more sightseeing," said the princess cheerily, and she got up. "Thank you for toasting the marshmallows. Maybe I'll come back and see you tomorrow."

"Yes, do that," answered the dragon, "if your mother will let you."

"Bye," called the Princess Georgiana.

"Bye!" shouted the dragon.

The princess set off down the hill.

*   *   *

She was back next morning.

"Hello!" she called loudly.

The dragon poked its head out of the cave.

"Oh, it's you."

"I came to ask you something."

"Well, ask me then," grumbled the dragon, "and hurry up about it."

"I told my mother about you and she asked if it's true that dragons have ugly great warts on their noses."

"Of course I don't!" snapped the dragon. "What a rude and stupid girl you are. You can see for yourself I haven't got warts. In fact, I'm considered very handsome as dragons go."

"People think *I'm* pretty, too," said the Princess Georgiana.

"*I* don't," remarked the dragon.

The Princess Georgiana ignored him and went on, "I told my mother about your gem collection. She said it couldn't be a very big one, the way I described it. It didn't sound to her as big as the treasure the other dragon's got over at Widdock Hill in the next kingdom."

"It's bigger and better," screeched the dragon. "How dare you say it's smaller? You are the most ignorant girl I ever met."

"Well, I'd sort of forgotten it by the time I got home," explained the princess, "so perhaps I didn't describe it to my mother properly."

"Go inside that cave and look again!" ordered the dragon.

The princess looked worried.

"I don't think I should."

"You must. I'm telling you to," snapped the dragon. "And when you've seen it again you can tell your mother the truth. Why, it's seven times as big as that gem collection of old One-Eye at Widdock's Hill. No comparison at all."

The princess went reluctantly into the cave.

Once she was inside she slipped to the back and whispered in Prince Blanziflor's ear.

"Did it work?"

The prince nodded.

Then he whispered back, "The baked beans were WON-DERFUL."

"Just do as I say and trust me," murmured the princess.

Blanziflor nodded.

The princess went back outside.

"You're right," she said, impressed. "It *is* enormous. I'd forgotten. I'll get on back home and tell my mother right away. 'Bye then."

"Oh, by the way," rumbled the dragon, "thank you for that advice about feeding the hostage. You should have seen his face when I gave him baked beans. He hated them."

"I'll bet he did," said the princess, and waving goodbye she set off down the hillside.

She spent the night camped about two miles away with Bucephalus. They built a fire together.

"My armour's getting heavy," complained the princess.

Bucephalus nodded sympathetically, as they stretched out beside each other and fell asleep.

Next day, the princess got up very early. She rode Bucephalus back to the bottom of the hill and tied him to the tree, out of sight. Then she checked her armour and equipment, slung her longbow on her back and went up the hill.

A short distance from the cave she stopped.

"Come out, you stupid old dragon," she shouted. "I'm

the Princess Georgiana and I've come to fight you and claim back my father's treasure. It's not yours. You stole it. You're nothing but a thief."

There was a low rumble and a roar from inside the cave. The ground shook.

The princess went several steps closer.

"You're afraid," she called. "You're too scared to fight me!"

A blast of flame came pouring out of the cave. Even from a distance the princess could feel the heat on her cheeks. She pulled down her heat proof vizor and, taking out her sword, she clashed it against a large rock.

"You're not a dragon. You're nothing but a baby."

There was a terrible howl from the cave. The dragon came roaring out.

"It's you!" it shrieked. "You wicked girl. I'll roast you alive."

And it breathed out a huge double jet of flame.

The Princess Georgiana hid behind a rock. She was terrified, but she was also very brave. Fumbling at her side, she unstrapped her fire extinguisher, then, poking her head out from behind the rock, she called, "Yah, yah, can't catch me!"

The dragon was enraged. It exhaled a mighty breath and shot out an even longer tongue of fire. Just as she felt the searing heat over her head, the princess raised the fire extinguisher and pressed the lever.

The dragon's fiery breath vanished. It coughed and

choked and spat. By now it was thoroughly angry and furious.

"You won't escape me," it bellowed and, rising on its hind legs with its wings outstretched, it showed its enormous talons. "I'll tear you to pieces!"

It was a terrifying sight. Georgiana felt as though she was having a nightmare.

"I must be calm and sensible," she whispered to herself, but her hands shook with fright. Trembling, she took out her catapult, spat on her hands for luck, and, with one deft move, popped a sharp stone in the sling and pulled it back.

The dragon came closer. Georgiana saw its terrible pointed teeth. She pulled the catapult sling tighter, took a deep breath and let fly. Twang!

The stone shot through the air and lodged straight in the dragon's forehead between the eyes. The dragon gave an earsplitting scream. Fiery vapour came pouring out of the wound and black blood spurted out of its mouth. It writhed and tossed and shook, then fell in a heap onto the ground.

The Princess Georgiana remembered what her old nanny had told her about dragons.

"They're very tricky things, dragons. Never let one fool you. Just when you think they're dead and done for, they jump up and catch you again."

So she went, very cautiously, just a little nearer. The dragon's eyes were closed and its body trembled.

"I'd better be on the safe side," thought the princess.

She fumbled under her armour and pulling out a box

of matches, took one out and struck it against her knee pads. It lit. Georgiana took a dead branch from the ground nearby and set fire to the end. Then she picked up her longbow, set the branch in like an arrow, took aim and fired the burning branch straight into the dragon's chest.

There was a tremendous explosion! A jet of flame shot into the air and enveloped the dragon. Boom! It frizzled up within a minute.

"Nanny was right then!" murmured the princess. "Dragons *do* have liquid gas instead of blood. How lucky I wasn't standing too close."

She went cautiously up to the crater in the ground where the dragon had been. There was nothing left but a heap of soot and ashes.

"Serves you right!" said the princess sternly. "You wicked dragon. Well, ex-dragon, I mean."

And she hurried up to the cave to tell Prince Blanziflor he was now free.

"You can come out," she called. "You're free. I've slain the dragon."

There was a little scuffling noise from the back of the cave.

"Are you sure?" whispered a frightened voice.

"Positive!"

"But I just heard a most terrible explosion."

"I know. It was me blowing up the dragon."

"Was it? I thought it was the dragon blowing up *you*."

The prince peeped cautiously out of the doorway, saw the dragon was gone, and stood blinking in the unaccustomed sunlight.

He looked at the princess. His lip trembled, he threw his arms round her neck and burst into tears.

"My heroine! How can I ever thank you enough?" he sobbed.

The Princess Georgiana patted him soothingly.

"Never mind," she said. "It's all over now. All we have to do is get you back to your mother's kingdom."

Prince Blanziflor wept harder.

"I haven't even got a horse. Mine bolted when it saw the dragon."

"We can both ride on mine," said the princess generously. And she led him over to the tree where Bucephalus was waiting.

Blanziflor climbed up on his back, and Princess Georgiana was just about to get up too when suddenly she stopped.

"Wait," she cried, and rushed off into the cave. She reappeared with a large piece of wood on which she wrote,

"PROPERTY OF THE PRINCESS GEORGIANA KEEP YOUR HANDS OFF!!!"

She propped it up at the cave entrance.

"We can come back later for the treasure," she explained.

"We?" asked Prince Blanziflor.

"Me and the palace guards," said the princess.

The prince was disappointed. "I thought you meant me."

"Do you want to come? I though you hated it here."

"It'd be different coming here with you, with no dragon," explained Blanziflor.

The princess smiled at him.

Prince Blanziflor took her hand.

"Will you marry me?" asked the princess.

Prince Blanziflor looked disappointed again.

"You're supposed to get down on one knee and ask me," he pointed out.

"As a matter of fact," snapped the princess, "*you're* supposed to do the asking." And she stamped off in a huff. The prince thought for a moment. Then he went running after her.

"Georgiana," he said in honeyed tones, "Georgiana. I love you. Will you marry me?"

The princess turned round.

"*You* haven't gone down on one knee, I notice," she said acidly.

Prince Blanziflor knelt down.

"PLEASE," he begged.

The Princess Georgiana looked severely at him.

"You were *very* rude to me just now."

"I'm sorry," said the prince. "I was still in a state of shock from the dragon and being in the cave so long and everything. And I think I was still a bit blinded by the light. *PLEASE*, Georgiana."

The princess gave a gracious smile.

"All right then, I will."

The prince cheered.

"But . . ." said the princess.

"Yes?"

"You can't just be king later on when we have our own kingdom. You have to take equal turns with me. A year each."

"A year each it is," agreed Blanziflor.

"And when we have royal babies you have to take turns at looking after them."

"I'd like that," said the prince. "And *you*, Georgiana, will have to help me mow the palace lawns and clean the royal carriages."

"But we've got fifteen gardeners," objected the princess.

"Well, if we get poor, you'll have to."

"All right," said the princess. "So it's all settled."

"Yes."

"By the way, Blanziflor . . ."

"Yes?"

"I love you too," said the princess. "And when I get home I'm having an octuple double strawberry-peanut-sausage-chocolate-crispy bacon-vanilla-peach-stardust ice-cream with treble flakes from my father's icecream machine. I really think I deserve it."

"I think you do, too," said the prince.

And he put his arm tenderly round her as they rode off together back to the palace.

The
ENCHANTED
TOAD

There was once a king who had a daughter called Princess Grizelda. Princess Grizelda was rather quiet and didn't say very much but she was very very stubborn and determined once she had decided on something.

The Queen, her mother, had left their home at the palace many years before, when Grizelda was a small girl, to seek her fortune as a racing driver, so the king had had to bring up his daughter himself.

"Grizelda," he said to her one day, "I have a serious problem to discuss with you. Come into the blue drawing room."

The Princess sighed, put down her bow and arrows and followed him.

"What is it, Papa?"

"Grizelda," said the king, "it's time you were married."

"But I'm only fourteen, Papa," protested the princess.

"What do you mean – 'only fourteen'?" said the king crossly. "Fourteen's quite old enough to be married."

"But I don't *want* to be marrried, Papa."

"Well, sooner or later you'll have to be," said the king, "so why not now?"

"I don't know if I ever want to be married, Papa."

"What nonsense!" shouted the king. "Everyone wants to be married. Why I was married at twenty and your mother was married at fifteen."

"I know, Papa," said the princess, "and when she was eighteen she went off to race cars and we haven't seen her since."

"Well, she always sends you a birthday present," said the king defensively.

"Yes, I know, but I'd rather *see* her sometimes."

"Grizelda," said the king, "you are not to talk about Mama. You know it only upsets me. I'm not going to listen if you do. And I want you, in fact, I'm ordering you, to start thinking about who you want to marry. Because if you don't come up with some good suggestions yourself, I shall have to choose for you."

And he stormed out of the blue drawing room.

"Oh dear," said Grizelda to herself, "Now I really *do* have a problem."

She thought about all the neighbouring princes but she really couldn't face the thought of marrying any of them.

*   *   *

"Well," asked the king at dinner, "have you decided, Grizelda?"

"Really, Papa, you only asked me to think about it five hours ago."

The king stamped his foot and his soup plate rattled.

"Five hours is long enough for anyone," he thundered.

"Not for me, Papa," said the princess calmly. "And you've spilt your soup."

"Oh, be quiet!" shouted the king and he slammed out of the royal dining room.

The princess ate the rest of her dinner in thoughtful silence.

Next day she had breakfast in her room, got dressed in her best golden dress and slipped outdoors in her blue silk cloak.

"Your Highness," said the Court Usher as she passed him on the stairs, "have you remembered that His Majesty has asked several kings and queens from neighbouring kingdoms to lunch with him today? He particularly wanted Your Highness to be present."

The princess nodded.

"Thank you for reminding me," she said, and to herself she thought, "He's asked them because he thinks they might be interested in marrying me off to one of their sons."

And she carried on downstairs even faster.

She stayed in the gardens for an hour or two, then slipped back into the palace and up to her bedroom

unnoticed. She had just enough time to sort out one or two things before lunch.

There was a blast of trumpets from downstairs.

"That'll be the heralds announcing the arrival of the other monarchs," said Princess Grizelda aloud and she smoothed her golden dress, picked up something in her hand and set off for the main staircase and the royal reception room.

"The Princess Grizelda," announced the Court Usher.

"My dear!" cried the king and he walked up and embraced her warmly. "Behave yourself, please," he muttered in her ear.

"I always do, Papa," said the princess.

"And this," announced the king, leading her forward, "is my daughter, Grizelda, my only child, who will, naturally, inherit the kingdom in due course and who, I really feel, is just of an age to be married."

The royal guests smiled at her. The princess smiled back. She took a deep breath.

"Papa," she said loudly, taking a step forward, "I've found a husband for myself."

"Really, Grizelda?" said the king. "I am surprised. And who is the lucky young man going to be?"

"It isn't a *young man*, Papa," said the princess. "I met him in the garden this morning and brought him in to lunch with me."

The king was curious.

"Let him come in!" he commanded, "so we can all see

this mysterious fellow. "Met him in the garden, indeed! These young girls are so fanciful."

The princess went out to the hallway, picked up a small box she had deposited there and carried it in.

"Well?" demanded the king. "Where is he then?"

The princess lifted the lid of the box.

"Here, Papa."

The king looked in the box.

"It's a toad!!"

"Yes, I know, Papa. I've fallen in love with it and I'm going to marry it."

"GRIZELDA!" thundered the king.

"Lunch is served, Sire," announced the footman appearing at the door.

One of the visiting kings leaned over to Grizelda's father and whispered in his ear, "I shouldn't discourage her too hard if I were you. It will almost certainly be a prince under enchantment."

The king was doubtful.

"Are you sure?"

"They always are," said the visiting king. "Let her have him on the table at lunch and have your Court Wizard change him back later on."

"What a splendid idea," said the king. "Thank you. I hadn't thought of that."

"There have been dozens of cases exactly like it," pointed out the visiting king.

So the Princess Grizelda took her toad in to lunch and it

sat by her golden plate as she fed it with tiny scraps of her own food.

The visitors left in the early afternoon. Grizelda shook hands with them all and smiled prettily. The toad looked at them with its unblinking eyes.

The king felt a light touch on his shoulder.

"Don't forget. Get the enchanter in right away," murmured his friend.

The king nodded.

"And many thanks," he said gratefully.

"Don't mention it," said the visiting king.

The princess took her toad into the library. She was examining its warts when the herald arrived with a message that she and the toad were wanted in the throne room.

"The throne room!" The princess was impressed. "Something special must be happening."

"His Majesty is in full regalia," announced the herald importantly.

"Really? It must be something vital then. I wonder what it can be?" said the princess, and picking up her toad she set off along the palace corridor.

The throne room door was opened by the Chief Usher. Inside the room were the King, the Lord Chamberlain, the Court Jester, the Chief Judge and the Court Enchanter. The Court Enchanter was considered to be one of the best wizards in the world. He was always going off to perform difficult spells or to change people back into their normal shapes or to magick someone or something somewhere.

People said he could conjure up all sorts of wonderful things and nobody wanted to get on the wrong side of him because it was reputed that he had once put a bad spell on someone who had offended him and caused lizards to jump out of her mouth every time she opened it.

Grizelda went into the room.

"Good afternoon, Papa," she greeted him, and she smiled and nodded at his retinue.

"Good afternoon, my dear," said the king and, looking at the toad, he said, obviously making a great effort, "and how is my future son-in-law this afternoon?"

"Oh, very well, thank you, Papa."

"Good," said the king.

"Would you like to stroke him, Papa?"

"No, no thanks!" said the king hastily. "Ah, I'm sure he's, ah, very, ah, friendly, yes, I'm sure he's got a wonderful nature and so on, but, ah, I don't think I'll stroke him just yet, thank you, Grizelda.

"Now," he went on, "the reason I've brought you down here is because I happen to believe your toad, that is, my son-in-law to be, is really a prince under enchantment."

The Princess Grizelda was very disappointed.

"Oh no, Papa, I hope not!"

"Now look here," said the king. "Don't be ridiculous, Grizelda. I mean you can get toads anywhere but princes are another thing altogether. I'll get you another toad as a wedding present if you want. And that's a promise. Now bring that toad over here and put him on the small table."

Grizelda put her toad down in front of the enchanter.

The enchanter looked at her with his piercing green eyes.

"Stand back, Your Highness," he ordered. Then, taking a huge red silk handkerchief from one pocket of his robe, and a wand from the other, he dropped the handkerchief over the toad, threw a powder from another pocket into a glass of water, poured the water over the handkerchief, then waved his wand over it, muttering strangely to himself all the time.

There was sudden flash of pink smoke and a dull boom, the handkerchief and the toad disappeared, and in its place stood a white rabbit.

The princess was overjoyed.

"A rabbit! Oh, Papa, how wonderful! I've always wanted a rabbit."

"Not for a *husband*!" bellowed the king, enraged.

And to the enchanter he said nastily, "You'll have to do something considerably better than that!"

The enchanter turned his piercing green eyes towards the king.

"Patience, Your Highness. These things are very skilled and take time."

"I can see that," said the king bitterly.

The enchanter pulled out another handkerchief, a blue one this time, and laid it over the rabbit.

"Oh no, please don't, please don't." The princess was distressed.

The enchanter put his hand deep in his robe, pulled out a tiny top hat, and presented it to her.

"Here you are," he said gravely. "Put your hand in there."

Grizelda could only get two fingers into the hat because it was so small. Feeling something soft and furry, she pulled at it.

Out popped the tiniest baby rabbit she had ever seen.

"For you," said the enchanter. "A present to make up for losing this one."

"Oh thank you!" cried Princess Grizelda and she put the baby rabbit back in the hat for safe keeping and put the hat in her pocket.

The enchanter was busy with his spell. He had taken out

a large book from behind the throne, a book Grizelda was
sure had never been there before, and was studying it
intently.

Suddenly he leaned forward towards the king.

"Excuse me, Your Majesty," he said, reached behind the
king's ear and pulled out a large lemon.

"Oh dear," he said, and reaching behind the king's other
ear, pulled out an enormous black spider.

"Stop it *at once!*" commanded the king. "And that's an
order."

"Sorry, Your Majesty," murmured the enchanter. "I just
thought you'd like to know they were there."

"Thank you for that consideration," said the king. "Now
get on with the job."

The enchanter plucked a star from out of the air above his head, laid it on the blue handkerchief, twirled three times round on his toes, and shouted "Abracadabra!"

There was a blinding flash of green light and, lo and behold, a beautiful red sportscar appeared before them.

"My gosh!" breathed Grizelda.

The Lord Chancellor leaned forward enviously. "I'd like that," he sighed.

The king looked very hard at the enchanter. "I see: a sportscar."

"Well, yes," said the enchanter. "I told Your Majesty these things take time."

"Look," said the king through clenched teeth, "I cannot

have a sportscar as a son-in-law. The princess cannot marry a *sportscar*."

His voice rose to a shriek. "WHOEVER HEARD OF A KINGDOM RULED BY A SPORTSCAR?"

"A passing bagatelle, Your Majesty," said the enchanter hastily. "We're almost there now."

"It's a very beautiful sportscar," pointed out the princess.

"Grizelda . . . ," said the king warningly.

The Lord Chamberlain broke in. "Your Majesty, the enchanter is about to try again."

"He'd better," said the king.

The enchanter took out a checked tablecloth from the back pocket of his robe and flung it over the sportscar.

The Lord Chamberlain sighed. "What a pity."

The king shot him a furious look.

The enchanter lifted three lizards out of a banqueting dish on the regalia table and laid them on the cloth. He took a vial of red liquid from his sleeve, shook it over the lizards and waved his wand low over them.

A tongue of flame shot into the air. Everybody screamed and jumped back.

The smoke cleared and there before them lay – a fish finger.

"NO, NO, NO, NO," groaned the king. "THERE IS NO SUCH THING AS A KINGDOM RULED BY A FISH FINGER! I'm *not* having a fish finger as a son-in-law. I'd rather have a toad. Take him away!" he shouted, pointing at the enchanter. "Off with his head and bring it to me on a plate! It'll be a pleasure, I can tell you."

"Papa!" The princess was deeply shocked. "What a *terrible* thing to say."

The enchanter burst into tears. He reached into his other sleeve and brought out a placard saying,

"WIFE AND SIX CHILDREN TO SUPPORT".

"You won't get my sympathy *that* way," said the king. "My mind is made up. Take him away!"

The Princess Grizelda jumped to her feet and stood in front of her father.

"I won't have it, Papa," she cried sternly. "This was all your idea in the first place and it wasn't even your toad. It was mine. Of course you're not going to chop off his head.

You're going to give him one last chance to succeed and if he doesn't, you're going to send him on a month's holiday."

"That's just encouraging him to fail," said the king.

"Honestly, Sire," said the enchanter, "it was just a temporary setback. I've prepared my next and final spell now. I *am* in the entertainment business, Sire, after all."

"Entertainment!" exploded the king. "You call this entertainment?"

"Stop it, at once, both of you," ordered the princess. And turning to the enchanter she said, "Would you please try again now?"

"And you'd better get it right this time," snorted the king.

"I will, " the enchanter assured them.

He pulled a purple silken cloth with golden stars on it from the Chief Judge's trouser leg and laid it over the fish finger. Then he reached inside his own mouth, pulled out a tonsil and laid that on the cloth.

"Yuk!" said the king. "How disgusting!"

"But effective, Sire," replied the enchanter. "And now, please, absolute silence."

He bent down on his knees, crossed his fingers, his toes, and his eyes and breathed on the tonsil.

The tonsil quivered and grew and grew. The purple cloth with golden stars rose and flapped and shook until it seemed to fill the room. There was a boom of thunder and a light like the sun dazzled them all.

"How beautiful!" murmured the princess to herself.

Suddenly there was a jolt and a bang and without warning they all flew up to the ceiling and fell to the ground again. The room grew dark.

"Sorry about this," came the enchanter's voice through the gloom. "We're nearly there."

A misty cloud was gathering in the middle of the room. A dim human shape was forming inside it.

The enchanter sighed inaudibly with relief, the king muttered aloud, "At last!"

And the Princess Grizelda said to herself, "I do hope he's nice and he likes having fun."

The cloud began to dispel, the light slowly returned to normal and the figure emerged more clearly until it stood visible to them all.

"GOOD HEAVENS!" bellowed the king. "It's Marguerite!"

"Hello, darling," said the figure.

"Mother!" shouted Grizelda and threw herself into the stranger's arms.

"And where have *you* been for the last eleven years then, if it's not a rude question?" asked the king.

"Oh, Arthur," said the queen, holding Grizelda tightly, "don't go on and on, please. I thought you'd be so pleased to see me again. I've been away seeking my fortune, of course. I'm an extremely famous racing driver."

"Well, I've never heard of you," announced the king, "and I've checked the racing lists every time there's been a Grand Prix."

"Oh, Arthur. Did you!" The queen was touched. "That is romantic of you."

The king blushed.

"But," went on the queen, "I raced under an assumed name of course, otherwise people might have thought my winning was favouritism. And, Grizelda," she continued, "it's so wonderful to see you at last, my darling. I've wanted and wanted to come back, but I knew I couldn't until I'd proved myself. And I've finally done it."

The Princess Grizelda clung tighter to her mother's neck.

"Oh, Mama, I'm so glad you're back at last."

"What I don't understand," said the king, "is if you've reached the peak of your career, what on earth you were doing in the palace garden disguised as a toad. And then to put me through that dreadful business of the rabbit and the sportscar and the fish finger! It's a wonder I'm not grey with worry and strain."

"Well, I couldn't help it," explained the queen. She turned to the enchanter. "It was a terribly strong spell. You did marvellously well to break it at all."

The enchanter looked modest.

"It was nothing, Your Highness."

"It was everything to *me*," the queen assured him. "I could have just about coped with spending the rest of my life as a pet rabbit or a sportscar and at least I would have been at the palace. But a fish finger! I ask you? Here one day and gobbled up the next. I was quite terrified. I was shaking in my breadcrumbs."

"Oh, Mama," breathed Grizelda, "just imagine if the enchanter had failed and we'd eaten you up for tea."

Her eyes filled with tears at the thought.

"Well, we didn't," said the king cheerfully, "so stop crying, Grizelda."

He came and put his arm round the queen and kissed her cheek.

"I'm so glad you've come back."

"I shall never go off again now, I can tell you," promised the queen, "though I had some fun while I was racing."

"Will you tell me all about it?" asked Grizelda eagerly.

"Later," promised the queen.

"We must have a banquet and a party to celebrate your return," said the king, "but there's still one thing I don't understand. How did you come to be a toad?"

"Well," explained the queen, "I was racing very well indeed and clearly I was going to win the major prize. The only person who was anywhere near as good as I was, was a driver who had been a wizard and had given it up for racing, but he was still not up to my standard. And when I had won the competition and it came to the presentation of the prizes, he was so jealous that he cast a spell over me and changed me into a toad, and it took me seven months to hop back here to the palace and then it wasn't till this morning, when Grizelda found me, that anyone noticed me at all, and, of course, you know the rest of the story."

"Amazing," said the king.

"That wizard should be punished," said the Chief Judge.

"He will be," promised the king. "I shall make a point of it."

"Well, if everyone is happy now," put in the enchanter, "I'd quite like to be getting off home to my own family . . ."

"Just a moment," said the king sternly. "You promised me a husband for the princess and I haven't got one. She can't marry her mother."

"With respect, Sire," said the enchanter, "*you* asked me if I could change a toad into a prince and I said I'd do my best. I rather thought," he went on huffily, "that I'd done better than my best, but of course if Your Majesty disagrees . . ."

"Absolutely. You've done *marvellously*," cried the queen, "and I shall personally see about a reward in due course."

The enchanter smiled gratefully.

"I still don't know how I'm going to get Grizelda a husband though," muttered the king.

"A husband!" The queen was incredulous. "What on earth does she want a *husband* for? She's only fourteen."

"I don't," put in Grizelda hastily.

"I should think *not*," said the queen. "I've never heard such nonsense. I married young, and look what happened to me. You're surely not encouraging her, Arthur?"

"Well, what else is she going to do?" asked the king defensively.

"What do you want to do, Grizelda?" asked her mother.

Grizelda thought for a bit.

"Well, Mama," she said finally, "what I'd like to do first is to stay here with you for a while and play with my rabbit, and the toad Papa has promised me, and then there is something I'd really like to do."

"And what is that?"

"I hope you won't think it's silly," said the princess, "but I'd simply *love* to be an astronaut. I've always wanted to be one."

"I've never heard of anything so ridiculous," said the king.

"I think it's a wonderfully exciting idea," said the queen, "and you should certainly be allowed to try it. And now, Arthur," she continued, turning to the king, "if it's possible, and I'm sure it should be, I'd love something to eat. I'm so sick of slugs and snails and worms."

"Oh, my dear," cried the king remorsefully, "of course, of course. I'm so sorry. I completely forgot about it in the shock of the moment. Yes. At once. Let's all three of us have a special celebration meal together tonight. I'm so delighted to have you back again."

"And so am I, Mama," murmured the Princess Grizelda, snuggling up to her mother.

"It seems to me," said the enchanter to himself, "that this time I've made an entirely satisfactory job of things."

And wrapping his cloak tightly round himself, he waved a hasty goodbye to everyone and slipped out of the palace off home to his own supper.